Wrath of the Atom Gods

The Lord Leader turned to Scientist Joquin. "Old man," he said curtly, "what is your purpose in defending the right to life of a freak?"

"Never before has a child of the atom gods been deliberately put to death. It was always assumed the gods had their own obscure purpose in creating monsters in human form. Do we dare test at this time that such is or is not the situation?"

The Lord Leader did not totally doubt their existence, but he was skeptical about their supernatural powers. "Do you really believe what you're saying?"

"As have so many others before me, I have visited the valleys where our gods are said to dwell. I saw from a safe distance behind lead embankments the incredible fires that still burn with unending fury in those fantastic deeps of Earth."

"'Truly,' I thought to myself, 'the gods, Uranium, Radium, Plutonium, and Ecks are the most powerful gods in the Universe. Surely,' I decided, 'no one in his right senses would do anything to offend them.'"

Before the Lord Leader could respond to this, from somewhere—it seemed terribly near—there was a sharp sound louder than the loudest thunder, followed half a minute later by a roar so loud, so furious, that the palace floor trembled. After a brief but not silent pause, from all directions came the sound of windows shattering. And then, that disturbance was overwhelmed by a third explosion, followed almost instantly by a fourth.

The last was so vast a sound that it was clear to everybody that the end of the world was imminent.

Clearly, the gods were displeased. Perhaps the child Clane should live . . .

Empire of the Atom

A. E. van Vogt

COLLIER BOOKS
Macmillan Publishing Company
New York

Maxwell Macmillan Canada
Toronto

Maxwell Macmillan International
New York   Oxford   Singapore   Sydney

Empire of the Atom is partially based upon material originally published in *Astounding Science Fiction* and copyrighted 1946, 1947 by Street & Smith Publications, Inc.

Collier Books
Macmillan Publishing Company
866 Third Avenue
New York, NY 10022

Maxwell Macmillan Canada, Inc.
1200 Eglinton Avenue East
Suite 200
Don Mills, Ontario M3C 3N1

Macmillan Publishing Company is part of
the Maxwell Communication Group of Companies.

Library of Congress Cataloging-in-Publication Data
van Vogt, A. E. (Alfred Elton), 1912–
    Empire of the atom / by A. E. van Vogt.
        p.   cm.
    ISBN 0-02-025991-3
    I. Title.
    PS3543.A6546E47   1993   92–28501   CIP
    813'.54—dc20

Macmillan books are available at special discounts for bulk purchases for sales promotions, premiums, fund-raising, or educational use.
For details, contact:

Special Sales Director
Macmillan Publishing Company
866 Third Avenue
New York, NY 10022

First Collier Books Edition 1993

10 9 8 7 6 5 4 3 2 1

Printed in the United States of America

To
Milo O. Frank

GENEALOGY
OF THE HOUSE OF LINN

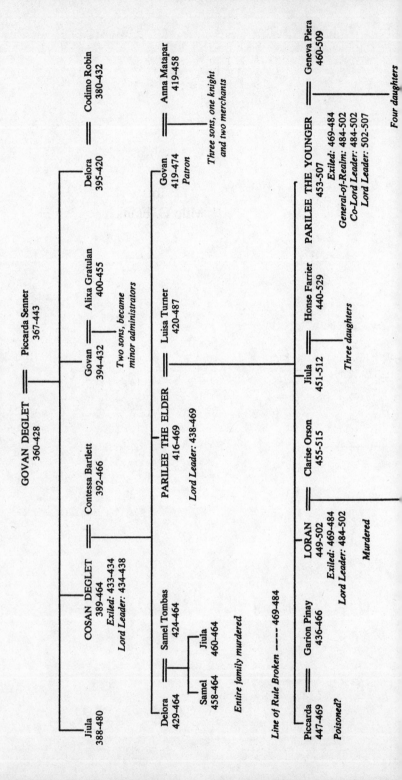

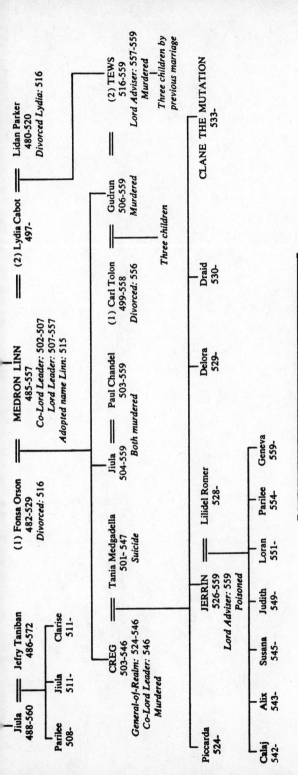

Jiula
488-560

Jefry Taniban
486-572

Parilee
508-

Jiula
511-

Clarise
511-

(1) Fonsa Orson
482-529
Divorced: 516

MEDRON LINN
485-557
Co-Lord Leader: 502-507
Lord Leader: 507-557
Adopted name Linn: 515

(2) Lydia Cabot
497-

Lidan Parker
480-520
Divorced Lydia: 516

(2) TEWS
516-559
Lord Adviser: 557-559
Murdered
Three children by previous marriage

CREG
503-546
General-of-Realm: 524-546
Co-Lord Leader: 546
Murdered

Tania Medgadella
501-547
Suicide

Jiula
504-559

Paul Chandel
503-559
Both murdered

(1) Carl Tolon
499-558
Divorced: 556

Gudrun
506-559
Murdered

Three children

CLANE THE MUTATION
533-

Piccarda
524-

JERRIN
526-559
Lord Adviser: 559
Poisoned

Lilidel Romer
528-

Draid
530-

Delora
529-

Calaj
542-

Alix
543-

Susana
545-

Judith
549-

Loran
551-

Parilee
554-

Geneva
559-

THE FOUNDATION OF LINN
Year 1 After Barbarism
About 12,000 A.D.

Two chieftains of the tribe of the Lake (Linnans) ended the period of barbarism on Earth and history began once more. The primitive city of Linn became the capital of the primitive state. By 200 A.B. the entire planet was under the control of the city-state of Linn. In 515 A.B. Medron Deglet adopted the name of the city-state of Linn as the surname of himself and his family.

Empire of the Atom

1

Junior scientists stood at the bell ropes all day, ready to sound forth the tidings of an important birth. By night, they were exchanging coarse jests as to the possible reason for the delay. They took care, however, not to bě overheard by seniors or initiates.

The expected child had actually been born a few hours after dawn. He was a weak and sickly fellow, and he showed certain characteristics that brought immediate dismay to the Leader household. His mother, Lady Tania, when she wakened, listened for a while to his piteous crying, then commented acidly: "Who frightened the little wretch? He seems already afraid of life."

Scientist Joquin, in charge of the delivery, considered her words an ill omen. He had not intended to let her see the monstrosity until the following day, but now it seemed to him that he must act swiftly to avert calamity. He hurriedly sent a dozen slave women to wheel in the carriage, ordering them to group around it in close formation to ward off any malignant radiation that might be in the bedroom.

Lady Tania was lying, her slim body propped up in bed, when the astonishing procession started to squeeze through the door. She watched it with a frown of amazement and then the beginning of alarm. She had patiently borne her husband four other children, and so she knew that what she was seeing was not part of any normal observance. She was not a soft spoken creature, and even the presence of a scientist in the room did not restrain her.

She said violently, "What is going on here, Joquin?"

Joquin fluttered his head at her in distress. Did she not realize that every ill-tempered word spoken at this period only doomed the child to further disasters? He noted, startled, that she was parting her lips to speak again— and, with a slight prayer to the atom gods, he took his life in his hands.

He took three swift strides towards the bed, and clapped his palm over her mouth. As he had expected, the woman was so astounded by the action that she did not immediately resist. By the time she recovered, and began to struggle weakly, the carriage was being tilted. And over his arm, she had her first glimpse of the baby.

The gathering storm faded from her blue eyes. After a moment, Joquin gently removed his hand from her mouth, and slowly retreated beyond the carriage. He stood there, quailing with the thought of what he had done, but gradually, as no verbal lightning struck at him from the bed, his sense of righteousness reasserted. He began to glow inwardly, and ever afterwards claimed that what he had done saved the situation as much at it could be saved. In the warmth of that self-congratulatory feeling, he almost forgot the child.

He was recalled by the Lady Tania saying in a dangerously quiet voice, "How did it happen?"

Joquin nearly made the mistake of shrugging. He caught himself in time, but before he could say anything, the woman said, more sharply: "Of course, I know it's due to the atom gods. But when do you think it happened?"

Joquin was cautious. The scientists of the temples had had much experience with atomic mutations, enough to know that the controlling gods were erratic and not easily pinned down by dates. Nevertheless, mutation did not occur after an embryo baby was a month in the womb and therefore a time limit could be estimated. Not after January, 533 A.B., and not before—he paused, recalling the approximate birth date of the Lady Tania's fourth child. He com-

10

pleted his reckoning aloud—"Certainly not before 529 After Barbarism."

The woman was looking at the child now, more intently. And Joquin, briefly, looked with her. He was surprised to realize how much he had not previously let himself see, but had simply glanced at in a scanning fashion. His new impression was even worse than it had been. The child had a big head for its frail body. Its shoulders and arms were the major visible deformity. The shoulders sloped down from the neck at a steep angle, making the body appear almost triangular. The arms seemed twisted, as if the bone—and the muscle and skin with it—had been given a full turn. It seemed as if each arm needed to unwind in order to be right. The boy's chest was extremely flat, and all the ribs showed through the stretched skin. The rib cage spread out in a web of bone that extended down too far for normalcy.

That was all. But it was evidently enough, for the Lady Tania swallowed visibly. Joquin, switching his gaze to her, thought he knew what was in her mind. She had made the mistake a few days before her confinement of boasting in a small company that five children would give her an advantage over her sister, Chrosone, who only had two children, and over her stepbrother, Lord Tews, whose acid-tongued wife had borne him three children. Now, the advantage would be theirs, for, obviously, she could have no more normal children, and they could overtake her, or surpass her at their leisure.

There would also be many witty exchanges at her expense. The potentialities for personal embarrassment were great.

Joquin read all that in her face as she stared with hardening eyes at the child. He said hurriedly: "This is the worst stage, Lady. Frequently, the result after a few months or years is reasonably—satisfactory."

He had almost said "human." He was aware of her gaze swinging towards him. He waited uneasily, but all

11

she said finally was, "Has the Lord Leader, the child's grandfather, been in?"

Joquin inclined his head. "The Lord Leader saw the baby a few minutes after it was born. His only comment was to the effect that I should ascertain from you, if possible, when you were affected."

She did not reply immediately, but her eyes narrowed even more. Her thin face grew hard, then harsh. She looked up at the scientist at last. "I suppose you know," she said, "that only negligence at one of the temples could be responsible."

Joquin had already thought of that, but now he looked at her uneasily. Nothing had ever been done about previous "children of the gods," but it had been growing on him that the Linns at least regarded this a special case. He said slowly, "The atom gods are inscrutable."

The woman seemed not to hear. Her cold voice went on, "The child will have to be destroyed, I suppose. But you may be sure that, within a month, there will be compensatory stretching of scientific necks such as the world has not seen in a generation."

She was not a pleasant person when aroused, the Lady Tania Linn, daughter-in-law of the Lord Leader.

It proved easy to trace the source of the mutation. The previous summer, Tania, tiring of a holiday on one of the family's west coast estates, returned to the capital before she was expected. Her husband, General-of-the-Realm Creg Linn, was having extensive alterations made to the Hill Palace. No invitation was forthcoming from her sister at the other end of the city, or from her stepmother-in-law, the stately wife of the Lord Leader. Tania, perforce, moved into an apartment in the Town Palace.

This assortment of buildings, though still maintained by the state, had not been used as a residence for several years. The city had grown immense since it was built, and long since the commercial houses had crowded around it. Due to a lack of foresight, by an earlier generation, title had not been taken to the lands surrounding the palace, and it had always been deemed unwise to seize them by force. There was one particularly annoying aspect of the failure to realize the profitable potentialities of the area. This was the scientists' temple that towered in the shelter of one wing of the palace. It had caused the Lady Tania no end of heartache the previous summer. On taking up residence, she discovered that the only habitable apartment was on the temple side, and that the three most beautiful plate windows faced directly on the blank lead walls of the temple.

The scientist who had built the temple was a member of the Raheinl group, hostile to the Linns. It had titillated the whole city when the site was made known. The fact that three acres of ground were available made the affront more obvious. It still rankled.

The agents of the Lord Leader discovered at the first investigation that one small area of the lead wall of the temple was radioactive. They were unable to determine the reason for the activity, because the wall at that point was of the required thickness. But the fact was what they reported to their master. Before midnight of the second day after the child was born, the decision was in the making.

Shortly before twelve, Scientist Joquin was called in and told the trend of events. Once more he took his life in his hands. "Leader," he said, addressing the great man direct, "this is grave error into which your natural irritation is directing you. The scientists are a group, who, having full control of atomic energy dispensation, have developed an independent attitude of mind, which will not take kindly to punishments for accidental crimes. My advice is, leave the boy alive and consult with the scientists' council. I will advise them to remove the temple of their own volition, and I feel sure they will agree."

Having spoken, Joquin glanced at the faces before him. And realized that he had made a mistake in his initial assumption. There were two men and three women in the room. The men were the grave, lean Lord Leader and

13

the plumpish Lord Tews, who was Lady Lydia's only son by her first marriage. Lord Tews was acting General-of-the-Realm in the absence of Lord Creg, Tania's husband, who was away fighting the Venusians on Venus.

The women present were the Lady Tania, who was still in bed, her sister, Chrosone, and the Lord Leader's wife, Lydia, who was stepmother-in-law to the two younger women. The Lady Tania and her sister were not on speaking terms, but they did maintain an indirect communication through Lord Tews. That individual managed his liaison role with an easy intelligence and—at least so it seemed to Joquin—genuine enjoyment.

Hopefully, Joquin watched the Lady Lydia, seeking in her face and attitude some indication of her purpose. He regarded her as a woman of enormous evil potential. Because of her, the pattern of behavior of the Linn family had radically altered. A handsome, middle-aged woman, with well-formed features, she was more dangerous than anything that crawled. Gradually, as the cunning pattern of her intrigue had spread octopus-like through the government, each person affected had in his own way learned how to deal with it. Counter-intrigues, schemes, constant vigilance, consciousness of unknown danger that might threaten or strike at any time—this had been the price. The sustained strain had hurt the Linn family. The poison was in them now, also. Tense and nervous, unhappy and vindictive, they were here in this room, their thoughts hidden but their motives predictable, and all because of the older woman.

Nevertheless, it was to the Lord Leader's wife that Joquin looked for a clue as to the finality of the decisions that had been made. Tall, thin, remarkably well preserved, she was the prime mover for destruction. If she had an opinion —and she *always* had an opinion—she would already have been working behind the scene. If she had managed to persuade her compromise-minded husband to take this specific action, then the stage was set for disaster.

Even as he divined from their manner that they had

called him for psychological reasons only, Joquin forced himself to assume that he was being consulted. The pretense was hard to maintain. He had the impression that they listened to his statement, as a matter of going through a form, but that actually little attention was paid to his words. Lord Tews glanced at his mother, a faint smile on his plumpish face. She half-lowered her eyelids, as if to hide the thoughts that were there. The two sisters remained frozen-faced, staring at Joquin. The Lord Leader ended the tension by nodding a dismissal to the scientist.

Joquin went out, quivering. He had the wild idea that he would send a warning to the endangered temple scientists. But he quickly abandoned that as hopeless. No message from him would be allowed out of the palace. He retired, finally, but he was unable to sleep. In the morning, the fearful rescript that he had visualized all through the night was posted on the military board, for all to read. Joquin blinked at it palely. It was simple and without qualification.

It commanded that every scientist of the Raheinl temple was to be hanged before dusk. The property was ordered seized, and the buildings razed to the ground. The three acres of temple ground were to be converted into a park.

It did not say that the park was to be added to the Town Palace of the Linns, though this later turned out to be the fact. The rescript was signed in the firm hand of the Lord Leader himself. Reading it, Joquin recognized that a declaration of war had been made against the power of the temple scientists.

2

The Scientist Alden was not a man who had premonitions. And certainly he had none as he walked slowly along towards the Raheinl temple. The morning glowed around him. The sun was out. A gentle breeze blew along the Avenue of Palms which stalked in stately fashion past his new home. His mind was the usual cozy kaleidoscope of happy reminiscences, and a quiet joy that a simple country scientist had in only ten years become the chief scientist of the Raheinl temple.

There was but one tiny flaw in that memory, and that was the real reason for his swift promotions. More than eleven years ago, he had remarked to another junior that, since the gods of the atom had yielded certain secrets of mechanical power to human beings, it might be worthwhile to cajole them by experimental methods into revealing others. And that, after all, there might be a grain of truth in the vague legends about cities and planets ablaze with atomic power and light. Alden shuddered involuntarily at the brief remembrance. It was only gradually that he realized the extent of his blasphemy. And when the other junior coolly informed him the following day that he had told the chief scientist—that had seemed like the end of all his hopes.

Surprisingly, it turned out to be the beginning of a new phase in his career. Within a month he was called for his first private conversation with a visiting scientist, Joquin, who lived in the palace of the Linns. "It is our policy," Joquin said, "to encourage young men whose thoughts do not move entirely in a groove. We know that radical ideas are common to young people, and that, as a man grows older, he attains a balance between his inward self and the requirements of the world. In other words," the scientist finished, smiling at the junior, "have your thoughts but keep them to yourself."

It was shortly after this that Alden was posted to the east coast. From there, a year later, he went to the capital. As he grew older, and gained more power, he discovered that radicalism among the young men was much rarer than Joquin had implied. The years of ascendancy brought awareness of the foolishness of what he had said. At the same time, he felt a certain pride in the words, a feeling that they made him "different" from, and so superior to, the other scientists. As chief, he discovered that radicalism was the sole yardstick by which his superiors judged a candidate for promotion. Only those recommendations which included an account of unusual thinking on the part of the aspirant, however slight the variance from the norm, were ever acted upon. The limitation had one happy effect. In the beginning, his wife, anxious to be the power behind the power at the temple, declared herself the sole arbiter as to who would be named for promotion. The young temple poets visited her when Alden was not around, and read their songs to her privately.

When they discovered that her promises meant nothing, their visits ceased. Alden had peace in his home, and a wife suddenly become considerably more affectionate . . .

His reverie ended for there was a crowd ahead, and cries and murmurs that had an unpleasant sound to them. He saw that people were swarming around the Raheinl temple. Alden thought blankly, "An accident?" He hurried forward, pushing through the outer fringes of the throng. He felt abrupt rage at the way individuals resisted his advance. Didn't they realize that he was a chief scientist? He saw mounted palace guardsmen urging their horses along the edge of the crowd a few score feet away, and he had his mouth open to call on them to assist him, when he saw

17

something that stopped his words in his throat. His attention had been on the temple proper. In his endeavor to move, his gaze flicked over the surrounding park.

Five of Rosamind's young poets were hanging from a tree limb at the edge of the temple grounds farthest from the temple. From a stouter tree nearby, six juniors and three scientists were still kicking spasmodically. As Alden stood paralyzed, a dreadful screaming came from four initiates whose necks were just being fitted with rope halters. The screaming ended, as the wagon on which they were standing was pulled from under them.

Scientist Alden tottered through the crowd before the Raheinl temple on legs that seemed made of dough. He bumped into people, and staggered like a drunken man, but he was only dimly aware of his gyrations. If he had been the only person in the group reacting, he would have been marked instantly, and dragged off to the gibbet. But the executions caught the throng by surprise. Each new spectator casually approaching to see what was going on suffered his own variation of tremendous shock. Women fainted. Several men were sick and others stood with glazed eyes.

As he approached one trailing end of the crowd, he was able to think again in flashes of insight. He saw an open gate; and he had darted through it, and was floating— that was the new sensation in his legs—through the underbrush, when it struck him that he was inside the grounds of the Town palace of Lord and Lady Creg Linn.

That brought the most terrible moment of the morning. Trapped, and of his own doing. He collapsed in the shelter of an ornamental shrub, and lay in a half faint of fright. Slowly, he grew aware that there was a long, low outhouse ahead, and that trees would shelter him most of the way. He recognized that he could not safely hope to return the way he had come, nor dared he remain where he was. He rose shakily to his feet, and the gods were with him. For he found himself shortly crouching in the long, narrow, hay storeroom adjoining the stables.

18

It was not a good hiding place. Its width was prohibitively confining, and only by making a tunnel in the hay near the door farthest from the stables did he manage to conceal himself. He had barely settled down when one of the stable doors a dozen feet to his right opened. A four-pronged fork flashed in a leisurely fashion, and withdrew transporting a bundle of hay. With a casual kick, the stable hand slammed the door shut, and there was the sound of retreating footsteps. Alden lay, scarcely breathing. He was just beginning to emerge from his bunk, when, *bang!* another door opened, and another fork gathered its hay, and departed.

A few minutes later there was a different kind of interruption. A young slave woman and a stable hand paused outside the frail barrier of wood that separated the hay section from the rest of the stable. The stable hand, evidently an army recruit and not a slave, said:

"Where do you sleep?"

"In the west slave pavilion." She sounded reluctant.

"What pallet?"

"Three."

He seemed to consider that. Then: "I'll come about midnight and crawl in with you."

"It's against the rules," the girl quavered.

"Let's not worry about rules," said the soldier roughly. "I'll see you."

The man walked off, whistling. The girl did not move— at least Alden heard nothing until rapid footsteps sounded. Then the young woman whispered briefly, as if telling the newcomer something. But her words were not audible to the listening scientist. Presently, however, another woman said:

"That's the second time since he arrived last week. The first time we substituted old Ella on him—he didn't seem to notice in the dark, and she's willing—but evidently he'll have to be dealt with. I'll pass the word on to the men." They separated, going in different directions.

Alden, who had been outraged by the soldier groom's

action, thought with equal outrage: "Why, those miserable slaves. They're actually planning against citizens."

It startled him, because it implied an understanding among slaves, whereby they defended themselves from particularly obnoxious owners. He had heard vaguely on previous occasions that small slave holders had become very careful as a result of assassinations. Here was partial evidence that the murderous legend was true.

Alden thought piously: "We must raise the moral standards of owners, and—" his eyes narrowed—"use force to break the secret slave organization. We can't have that kind of nonsense."

His rage departed instantly, as a door opened a hundred feet away. He ducked instinctively—and gave no further thought to the slave problem.

Despite the nervous shocks, by noon his mind had almost resumed functioning. He had his first theory as to why he had escaped the round-up that had caught the others. Only two weeks before, he had moved to his new residence on the Avenue of Palms. The soldiers must have proceeded to his old address, and then had to cross the city to his new home, with the result that he had left the house by the time they arrived.

Of such tenuous fabrics the patterns of his escape were woven. Alden shivered, and then, slowly, anger built up inside him, the deadly, gathering anger of a man wrongly persecuted. It was a fury that braced him for eventualities, and he was able at last to think with clear-cut logic of what he must do. Obviously, he could not remain within the grounds of the Town palace. Odd little memories came to his aid, things he had observed in earlier years without being aware that he did so. He recalled that every few nights hay ricks turned into the palace gates. Judging by the emptiness around him, a new supply must be almost due. He must leave before the afternoon was out.

He began to struggle along the line of hay to the right. There was a gate on that side, and he remembered having once glimpsed the stables through it while taking a walk.

By sneaking out of the end door and around the side of the stable, and then through *that* gate— If only he could find another set of clothes— Surely, there would be work clothes hanging up in the stables, preferably, in view of the long hair that scientists affected, a woman's overdress—

He found what he wanted in the right end of the stable, which was devoted to milk cows. The animals and he were quite alone while he arrayed himself in the raiment that the milkmaids pulled over their pretty dresses when they did their chores.

The Town Palace, after its brief flurry the year before as a Linn residence, had reverted swiftly to its role of agricultural, industrial and clerical center. There were guards within sight of the gate, but they did not bother to question a rather stocky woman slave, who went out with a decisive manner as if she had been sent on an errand by a superior.

It was late afternoon when Alden approached the Covis temple from the rear. He grew jittery as its leaden walls loomed up before him. His fear was that at this moment when safety was in sight, something would happen. He knocked timidly on one of the small back entrances, and waited, trembling.

The door opened suddenly; but he was so tense that he responded instantly, and stepped past the astonished junior who was there, into the shadows of the unlit corridor.

Not until he had jerked the door from the other's grip, and closed it—so that they stood in almost total darkness— did Alden reveal his identity to the startled young man.

3

Medron Linn, the Lord Leader, walked along a street of the city of Linn. His ventures into the town had become rarer in recent years, but as in the past he felt both interested and excited. As always he had a specific purpose. Only thus could he justify to himself the time and effort involved.

He had his normal quota of guards with him, but they were specially trained for these private wanderings; and so like soldiers on leave they made their way behind him or ahead of him as if they had no interest in the lean, pale, flint-faced man whose lightest command was law on Earth and on portions of several planets.

The Lord Leader sought out the most densely populated market areas, with their bright wares. The sight of so much color reminded him of his younger days, when all this part of the city had been drab and unpainted, and the craftsmanship behind each product low-grade. The traders had grumbled and raged when, in the early days of his power, he had decreed that the choice locations would be available only to those who were willing to paint them and maintain them, and who were willing to carry only better quality goods. It was a forgotten crisis. Under the stress of competition, the gaily decorated buildings had inspired an improvement in the appearance of all the stalls; and the superior quality of the merchandise sold had brought about a considerable increase in variety as well.

The Lord Leader Linn had to force his way among the throngs of buyers and sellers. The markets were crowded with people from the hills and from across the lake, and there was the usual pack of wide-eyed primitives from the other planets. At no time during the afternoon was it difficult to start a conversation.

He talked only to people who showed no sign of recognizing as their ruler the unshaven man in the uniform of a private soldier. It didn't take long to realize that the thousand persuasive men he had sent out to argue his side of the hangings were doing yeoman service. No less than seven approached him, and he permitted three of these to engage him in conversation. All three made skillful propaganda remarks. And the five farmers, three merchants and two laborers to whom he talked, subsequently answered his rough criticism of the Lord Leader with pro-government catchphrases they could only have heard from his own men.

It was gratifying, he told himself, that the first crisis he had forced was turning out so well. The Linnan empire was only a generation out of the protracted civil war that had brought the Linn family to a secure leadership. His tax collectors were still finding the returns lean. One of the reasons was the financial drain on the country by the temples. The scientists had the people in a thrall which— it seemed to the Lord Leader—could not possibly have any counterpart in history. Certain temple rites were hypnotic in nature, and there were trained men to suggest the exact amount of the contribution desired. Thousands of women, particularly, were so caught by such devices that it was necessary for the temples themselves to urge restraint upon them, lest they give all their possessions. The men, being often at war, were not so obsessed. Upon this vast income, the temples maintained a horde of scientists, seniors, juniors, and initiates. So enormous was this temple army that almost every family had at least one relative who was "studying" to become a scientist.

It had seemed to the Lord Leader—and he had not really needed Lydia to point it out—that an attempt must be made to break the hypnotic dominance involved. Until that happened, the strain on the economy would continue, and prosperity and wealth would only grow at a minimum rate. Trade had revived in Linn itself, but it was making much slower recovery in other cities, which were not favored by special exemptions.

Several wars of conquest were under way, three of them on Venus against the Venusian tribes. The goal of unification of the solar system, which he had set himself, required that those expeditions be maintained, regardless of cost. Something—it seemed to the Lord Leader—had to be sacrificed. Something big. He had selected the temples, as the only real rivals to the government in terms of their total annual income.

The Lord Leader paused before the open air shop of a dealer in ceramics. The man had the Linnan cast of feature and was obviously a citizen, or he wouldn't be in business. Only the opinions of the citizens mattered. This one was in the throes of making a sale. While he waited, the Lord Leader thought again of the temples. It seemed clear that the scientists had never recovered the prestige they had lost during the civil war. With a few exceptions they had supported Raheinl until the very day that he was captured and killed. The scientists promptly and collectively offered an oath of allegiance to the new regime, and he was not firmly enough entrenched in power to refuse. He never forgot, however, that their virtual monopoly of atomic energy had nearly re-established the corrupt republic. And that, if they had succeeded, it was he who would have been executed.

The merchant's sale fell through. He walked over grumpily to his potential new customer but at that moment the Lord Leader noticed a passerby had paused, and was staring at him with half recognition. The Lord Leader without a word to the merchant turned hastily, and hurried along the street into the gathering dusk.

The members of the Scientists Council were waiting for him when, satisfied that his position was unassailable, he returned finally to the palace.

It was not an easygoing gathering. Only six of the seven

members of the council of scientists were present. The seventh, the poet and historian, Kourain, was ill, so Joquin reported, with fever. Actually, he had suffered an attack of acute caution on hearing of the hangings that morning, and had hastily set out on a tour of distant temples.

Of the six, at least three showed by their expressions that they did not expect to emerge alive from the palace. The remaining three were Mempis, recorder of wars, a bold, white-haired old man of nearly eighty; Teear, the logician, the wizard of arithmetic, who, it was said, had received some of his information about complicated numbers from the gods themselves; and, finally, there was Joquin, the persuader, who, for years, had acted as liaison between the temple hierarchy and the government.

The Lord Leader surveyed his audience with a jaundiced eye. The years of success had given him a sardonic mien, that even sculptors could not eradicate from his statues without threatening the resemblance between the referent and the reality. He was about fifty years old at this time, and actually in remarkably good health despite his thinness. He began with a cold, considered and devastating attack on the Raheinl temple. He finished that phase of his speech with: "Tomorrow, I go before the Patronate to justify my action against the temple. I am assuming that they will accept my explanation."

For the first time, then, he smiled, bleakly. No one knew better than he or his audience that the slavish Patronate dared not even blink in a political sense without his permission. "I am assuming it," he went on, "because it is my intention simultaneously to present a spontaneous petition from the temples for a reorganization."

The hitherto silent spectators stirred. The three death-expecting members looked up with a vague hope on their faces. One of the three, middle-aged Horo, said eagerly, "Your excellency can count on us for—" He stopped because Mempis was glaring at him, his slate-blue eyes raging. He subsided, but gradually his courage returned. He had made his point. The Lord Leader must know that *he* was

25

willing. He experienced the tremendous inner easing of a man who had managed to save his own skin.

Joquin was saying suavely, "As Horo was about to state, we shall be happy to give your words a respectful hearing."

The Lord Leader smiled grimly. But now he had reached the crucial part of his speech, and he reverted to legalistic preciseness. The government—he said—was prepared at last to split the temples into four separate groups as had been so long desired by the scientists. (This was the first they had heard of the plan, but no one said anything.) As the scientists had long urged, the Lord Leader went on, it was ridiculous that the four atom gods, Uranium, Plutonium, Radium and Ecks should be worshiped in the same temples. Accordingly, the scientists would divide themselves into four separate organizations splitting the available temples evenly among the four groups.

Each group would give itself to the worship of only one god and his attributes, though naturally they would continue to perform their practical functions of supplying transmuted god-power to all who sought to purchase it under the government regulations. Each group would be headed, not by a council of equals as was the temple system at present, but by a leader for whom an appropriate title must be selected. The four separate temple leaders would be selected for life by a joint committee of government and temple delegates.

There was more, but they were details. The council had its ultimatum. And Joquin at least cherished no illusions. Four temple groups, fighting for adherents, each ruled by a willful scientist, responsible to no one except perhaps the Lord Leader, would end forever any hopes the more enlightened scientists entertained. He personally regarded the temples as the repositories of learning, and he had his own dreams as to the role the temples might play at some future time. He rose now hastily, lest one of the fearful councilors should speak first. He said gravely, "The council will be very happy to consider your offer, and feels itself privileged to have in the government a lord who devotes his obviously valuable time to thoughts about the welfare of the temples. Nothing could—"

He had not really expected to manage a postponement. And he didn't. He was cut off. The Lord Leader said with finality, "Since I am personally making the announcement in the Patronate chamber tomorrow, the Scientists Council is cordially invited to remain in the palace to discuss details of reorganization. I have assumed this will require anywhere from a week to a month, or even longer, and I have had apartments assigned for your use."

He clapped his hands. Doors opened. Palace guards came in. The Lord Leader said, "Show these honored gentlemen to their quarters."

Thus was the council imprisoned.

On the fourth day, the baby was still alive. The main reason was that Tania could not make up her mind. "I've had the burden of pregnancy and the turmoil of birth," she said savagely, "and no woman in her right mind nullifies that easily. Besides—" She stopped there. The truth was that, in spite of innumerable disadvantages, she could imagine certain uses for a son whom the gods had molded in their peculiar fashion. And in this regard, the urgings of Joquin were not without their effect. Joquin spent most of the fourth morning on the subject.

"It is a mistake," he said, "to assume that all the children of the gods are idiots. That is an idle talk of the witless mob, which pursues these poor creatures along the street. They are not given an opportunity for education, and they are constantly under pressures so great that it is little wonder few of them ever attain the dignity and sense of mature development." His arguments took on a more personal flavor. "After all," he said, softly, "he is a Linn. At worst, you can make of him a trustworthy aide, who will not have the same tendency to wander off to live his own life as will your normal children. By keeping him discreetly in the background you might acquire that best of all possible slaves, a devoted son."

27

Joquin knew when to stop pressing. The moment he noticed from the thoughtful narrowing of the woman's eyes that his arguments were weighing with her, he decided to leave her to resolve the doubts that still remained. He withdrew smoothly, and attended the morning court of the Lord Leader—and there once more urged his suit.

The great man's eyes were watchful as Joquin talked. Gradually, his satiric countenance grew puzzled. The Lord Leader interrupted at last. "Old man," he said curtly, "what is your purpose in thus defending the right to life of a freak?"

Joquin had several reasons, one of them almost purely personal, and another because he believed that the continued existence of the baby might, however slightly, be an advantage to the temples. The logic of that was simple. The baby's birth had precipitated a crisis. Its death would merely affirm that crisis. Conversely, if it remained alive, the reason for the ferocious reaction of the Linns would be negated to some small degree.

He had no intention of stating that particular reason, and he did not immediately mention his personal hope about the baby. He said instead, "Never before has a child of the gods been deliberately put to death. It was always assumed the gods had their own obscure purpose in creating monsters in human form. Do we dare test at this time that such is or is not the situation?"

It was an argument that made the other man stare in astonishment. The wars the Lord Leader had fought had thrown him into contact with advanced thinkers and skeptics on several planets, and he had come to regard the gods as a means of keeping his rebellious subjects under control. He did not totally doubt their existence but he was skeptical about their supernatural powers. "Do you really believe what you're saying?" he asked.

The question made Joquin uncomfortable for there was a time in his life when he had believed nothing. Slowly, however, he had been half convinced that the mighty invisible force given forth by the tiniest radioactive substance could have no other explanation. He said carefully: "In

28

my travels as a young man, I saw primitive tribes that worshipped rain gods, river gods, tree gods and various animal gods. And I saw more advanced races, some of them here on Earth, whose deity was an invisible omnipotent being who lives somewhere in space in a place called heaven. All these things I observed, and in a similar fashion I listened to each group's particular account of the beginning of the Universe. One story has it that we all came from the mouth of a snake. I have seen no such snake. Another story is that a great flood deluged the planets, though how this could have been done with the available water, I do not know. A third story is that man was created from clay and woman from man."

He looked at his hearer. The Lord L e a d e r nodded. "Continue."

"I have seen people who worshipped fire, and I have seen people who worshipped water. And then, as have so many others before me, I finally visited the valleys where our own gods are said to dwell. I discovered their residences on every planet, vast, desolate areas miles deep and miles long and wide. And in these areas, I saw from a safe distance behind lead embankments the incredible bright fires that still burn with unending fury in those fantastic deeps of Earth.

" 'Truly,' I thought to myself, 'the gods, Uranium, Radium, Plutonium and Ecks are the most powerful gods in the Universe. Surely,' I decided, 'no one in his right senses would do anything to offend them.' "

The Lord Leader, who had also examined some of the homes of the gods in the course of his peregrinations, said only, "Hm-m-m!"

He had no time for further comment. From somewhere —it seemed terribly near—there was a sharp sound louder than the loudest thunder that had ever bellowed from the skies. It was followed, half a minute later, by a roar so loud, so furious, that the palace floor trembled.

There was a pregnant pause, not silent. From all directions came the sound of windows shattering with a thousand tinkling overtones. And then, that disturbance was overwhelmed by a third explosion, followed almost instantly by a fourth.

This last was so vast a sound that it was clear to everybody that the end of the world was imminent.

4

When Alden entered the great Covis temple on the afternoon of the third day after the birth of the Linn baby, he was a tired, hungry man. But he was also a hunted man with the special thoughts of the fugitive. He sank into the chair that was offered by the junior. And while the young man was still in process of realizing the situation, Alden ordered him to inform no one of his presence except Horo, chief scientist of the Covis temple.

"But Horo is not here," the junior protested. "He has but just now departed for the palace of the Leader."

Alden began briskly to remove his female disguise. His weariness flowed from him. Not here, he was thinking gleefully. That meant *he* was the senior scientist in the temple until Horo returned. For a man who had as many thoughts as he had during the afternoon, that was like a reprieve. He ordered that food be brought him. He took possession of Horo's office. And he asked questions.

For the first time, he learned the only reason so far made public for the executions at the Raheinl temple. Alden pondered the reason throughout the early evening, and the more he thought the angrier he grew. He was vaguely aware that his thinking was on a very radical plane, if not heretical; and yet, paradoxically, he felt mortified that the gods had been so profoundly insulted in their temples. Somehow, with a crystalline certainty—that, yet, had in it no disbelief—he knew that they would not show their displeasure of their own volition. The thoughts of a fugitive tended automatically towards such practical convictions. Before the evening was half through, he was examining the possibilities.

From time immemorial the gods had favored certain processes. Commanding officers and other legal owners of spaceships brought ingots of iron to the temples. The ceremonial and money preliminaries being completed, the iron was then placed in close proximity to the uncovered god-stuff for one day exactly. After four days, one for each god, the power of the god-stuff was transmitted to the ingot. It was then removed by the offerer to his ship where, with simple ceremonials, it was placed in metal chambers—which any metal worker could make—and by the use of what was known as a photoelectric cell—a device also known from very early times, like fire and sword and spear and bow—an orderly series of explosions could be started and stopped at will.

When enough of these metal chambers were used, the largest ships that could be constructed by man were lifted as easily as if they were made of nothingness. From the beginning of things, the god-stuff in all the temples had been kept in four separate rooms. And the oldest saying in history was that when the gods were brought too close together, they became very angry indeed.

Alden carefully weighed out a small quantity of each type of god-stuff. Then he had four juniors carry a metal chamber from the testing cavern into the garden at the rear of the temple. At this point it struck him that other temples should participate in the protest. He had learned that six of the seven members of the Scientists Council were still at the palace, and he had a rather strong suspicion as to their predicament.

Writing from Horo's ornate office, he *ordered* the acting chiefs of the temples of the absent councilors to do exactly

31

what he was doing. He described his plan in detail, and finished: "High noon shall be the hour of protest." Each letter he sent by junior messenger.

He had no doubts. By noon the following day he had inserted his grains of uranium, radium, plutonium and ecks into the photoelectric relay system. From what he decided was a safe distance, he pressed the button that clicked over the relays in order. As the wonderful and potent ecks, joined the "pile," there was an explosion of considerable proportions. It was followed swiftly by three more explosions. Only two of the temples disregarded the commands of the fugitive. They were the fortunate ones. The first explosion blew half the Cov's temple into dust, and left the remnant a tottering shambles of dislodged masonry and stone.

No human being was found alive in any of the four temples. Of Alden there was not even a piece of flesh or a drop of blood.

By two o'clock mobs were surging around the foot of the palace hill. The palace guard, loyal to a man, held them off grimly, but retreated finally inside the gates, and the household of the Leader prepared for a siege.

When the pandemonium was at its height half an hour later, Joquin, who had been down in the city, returned by a tunnel that ran through the hill itself, and asked permission to speak to the mob. Long and searchingly, the Lord Leader looked at him. Then finally, he nodded. The mob rushed at the gates when they opened, but spearmen held them back. Joquin pressed his way out. His was a piercing rather than a deep voice, but the rostrum that jutted out from the hill was skillfully constructed to enable a speaker to address vast throngs through a series of megaphones.

His first act was to take the ribbons out of his hair, and let it down around his shoulders. The crowd began to shout: "Scientist. It's a scientist."

Joquin raised his hand. And the silence he received was evidence to him at least that the riots were about to end. The crowd was controllable.

On his own part, he had no illusions as to the importance

32

of this mob attacking the palace. He knew that carrier pigeon messages had been dispatched to the three legions camped just outside the walls of the city. Soon, a disciplined force would be marching through the streets, paced by cavalry units made up of provincial troops, whose god was a giant mythical bird called Erplen. It was important that the crowd be dispersed before those trained killers arrived on the scene.

"People of Linn," he said in a clear, confident voice, "you have today witnessed a telling proof of the power of the gods."

Cries and groans echoed his words. Then again, silence. Joquin continued, "But you have misread the meaning of the signs given us today."

This time, only silence greeted his words. He had his audience.

"If the gods," he said, "disapproved of the Lord Leader, they could just as easily have destroyed his palace as they actually did destroy four of their own temples. It is not the Lord Leader and his actions to which the gods objected. It is that certain temple scientists have lately tried to split up the temples into four separate groups, each group to worship one of the four gods only. That and that alone is the reason for the protest which the gods have made today."

There were cries of, "But your temple was among those destroyed."

Joquin hesitated. He did not fancy being a martyr. He had seen two of the letters Alden had written—to the two temples which had not obeyed the instructions—and he had personally destroyed both letters. He was not sure how he ought to rationalize the fact that a purely mechanical union of god-stuff had produced the explosions. But one thing at least was certain. The gods had not objected to their status of being worshipped four in one temple. And since that status was the only one that made it possible for the scientists to remain strong, then what had happened *could be* the gods' way of showing that it was their purpose, also.

Joquin recognized uneasily that his reasoning was a form of sophistry. But this was no time to lose faith. He bowed his head before the shouting, then looked up. "Friends," he said soberly, "I confess I was among those who urged separate worship. It seemed to me that the gods would welcome an opportunity to be worshipped each in his own temple. I was mistaken."

He half turned to face the palace, where far more important ears were listening than any in the crowd below. He said, "I know that every person who, like myself, believed the separatist heresy is now as convinced as I am that neither the four gods or their people would ever stand for such blasphemy. And now, before there is any more trouble, go home, all of you." He turned and walked slowly back into the palace grounds.

The Lord Leader was a man who accepted necessities. "There remains one undetermined question," he said later. "What is your real reason for keeping my daughter-in-law's baby alive?"

Joquin said simply, "I have long wanted to see what would happen if a child of the gods is given a normal education and upbringing."

That was all he said. It was enough. The Lord Leader sat with eyes closed, considering the possibilities. At last, slowly, he nodded his head.

5

Even as a baby, Clane had the feeling: *I'm not wanted. Nobody likes me.*

The slave women who tended his needs reflected in their

handling of him the antagonism of the parents. They were extremely aware that the mother and father seldom visited their new baby. For hours, on occasion, the tiny mutation had no one near it. And when his attendants subsequently found him wallowing in the wet and filthy cot, they were not inclined to be patient.

Hands capable of tenderness were somehow rougher when they touched him. And a thousand moments of ungentle treatment communicated to his muscles and his nerves, and became a part of his awareness of his environment. He learned to cringe as a baby, and he cringed as a toddler.

Oddly, when words began to make sense, there was for a while a change in his condition. Innocently, he said things to Joquin which gave that individual his first realization that the slaves were disobeying his instructions. A few questions each visit sharpened the picture to the point where the offending slaves discovered that the end result of unwise action or comments might well be a whipping. Men and women both learned the hard way that even defenseless babies grow older and show evidence of the treatment they have received.

However, the youngster's developing ability to understand had its drawbacks. Somewhere between the ages of three and four, Clane realized that he was different. Enormously, calamitously different. Between four and six, his sanity suffered collapse after collapse, each time to be slowly built back again by the aging scientist. Presently, the scientist Joquin realized that more drastic action was necessary if the boy's reason were to be saved.

"It's the other children," Joquin, white with fury, told the Lord Leader one day. "They torment him. They're ashamed of him. They defeat everything I do."

The Linn of Linn gazed curiously at the temple man. "Well, so am I ashamed of him, ashamed of the very idea of having such a grandson." He added: "I'm afraid, Joquin, your experiment is going to be a failure."

It was Joquin, now, who stared curiously at the other. In the six years that followed the crisis of the temples of the atom gods, he had come to have a new and more favorable regard for the Lord Leader. During those years it had occurred to him for the first time that here was the greatest civil administrator since legendary times. Something, also, of the man's basic purpose—unification of the empire—had shown occasionally through the bleak exterior with which he confronted the world. Here was a man, moreover, who had become almost completely objective in his outlook on life. That was important right now. If Clane were to be saved, the cooperation of the ruler of Linn was essential. The Lord Leader must have realized that Joquin's visit had a specific objective. He smiled grimly.

"What do you want me to do? Send him to the country where he can be brought up in isolation by slaves?"

"That," said Joquin, "would be fatal. Normal slaves despise the mutations as much as do freedmen, knights and patrons. The fight for his sanity must be made here in the city."

The other was suddenly impatient. "Well, take him away to the temples where you can work on him to your heart's content."

"The temples," said Joquin, "are full of rowdy initiates and juniors."

The Lord Leader glowered. He was being temporized with, which meant that Joquin's request was going to be difficult to grant. The entire affair was becoming distasteful. "I'm afraid, old man," said the Lord Leader gravely, "you are not being sensible about this matter. The boy is like a hothouse plant. You cannot raise the children of men that way. They must be able to withstand the rough and tumble of existence with their fellows even when they are young."

"And what," flashed Joquin, "are these palaces of yours but hothouses where all your youngsters grow up sheltered from the rough and tumble of life out there?"

The old scientist waved his hand towards the window that opened out overlooking the capitol of the world. The Leader smiled his acceptance of the reality of the comparison. But his next words were pointed.

"Tell me what you want. I'll tell you if it can be done."

Joquin did not hesitate. He had stated his objections, and, having eliminated the main alternatives, he recognized that it was time to explain exactly what he wanted. He did so, succinctly. Clane had to have a refuge on the palace grounds. A sanctuary where no other children could follow him under penalty of certain punishment.

"You are," said Joquin, "bringing up all your male grandchildren on your grounds here. In addition, several dozen other children—the sons of hostages, allied chiefs and patrons—are being raised here. Against that crowd of normal, brilliant boys, cruel and unfeeling as only boys can be, Clane is defenseless. Since they all sleep in the same dormitory, he has not even the refuge of a room of his own. I am in favor of his continuing to eat and sleep with the others, but he must have some place where none can pursue him."

Joquin paused, breathless, for his voice was not what it had been. And, besides, he was aware of the tremendousness of the request. He was asking that restrictions be put upon the arrogant, proud little minds and bodies of the future great men of Linn—patrons, generals, chieftains, even Lord Leaders of twenty, thirty, forty years hence. Asking all that, and for what? So that a poor wretch of a mutation might have the chance to prove whether or not he had a brain.

He saw that the Lord Leader was scowling. His heart sank. But he was mistaken as to the cause of the expression. Actually, he could not have made his request at a better time. The day before, the Lord Leader, walking in the grounds, had found himself being followed by a disrespectful, snickering group of young boys. It was not the first time, and the memory brought the frown to his face.

He looked up decisively and said, "Those young rascals need discipline. A little frustration will do them good. Build your refuge, Joquin. I'll back it up for a while."

The palace of the Leader was located on Capitoline Hill. The hill was skilfully landscaped. Its grounds were terraced and built up, be-gardened and be-shrubbed until the original hill was almost unrecognizable to old-timers like Joquin.

There was a towering rock on a natural peak at the west end of the grounds. To reach it one followed a narrow path up a steep slope, and then climbed the steps that had been cut into the solid rock to the top of the rock itself.

The rock was bare until Joquin took it over. Swiftly, under his direction, slaves carried up soil, and slave gardeners planted shrubs, grass and flowers, so that there might be protection from the hot sun, a comfortable green on which to stretch out and an environment that was beautiful and colorful. He built an iron fence to guard the approaches to the pathway, and at the gate stationed a freedman who was six feet six inches tall and broad in proportion. This man had a further very special qualification in that a child of the gods had also been born to his wife some four years before. The big man was a genial, friendly individual who prevented the more rowdy boys from following Clane by the simple act of wedging his great body into the narrow gate.

For weeks after the aerie was ready, and the restriction imposed, the other children railed and shrieked their frustration. They stood for hours around the gate tormenting the guard, and yelling threats up to the rock. It was the imperviousness of the always friendly guard that baffled them in the end. And at long last the shivering boy in the aerie had time to become calm, to lose that sense of imminent violence, and even to acquire the first feeling of security. From that time on, he was ignored. No one played with him, and, while their indifference had its own quality of cruelness, at least it was a negative and passive attitude. He could live his private life.

His mind, that wounded, frightened, and delicate complex of intellect and emotion, came slowly out of the darkness into which it had fled. Joquin lured it forth with a thousand cunnings. He taught it to remember simple poetry. He told the boy stories of great deeds, great battles, and many of the fairy tales currently extant. He gave him at first carefully doctored but ever more accurate interpretations of the polit-

38

ical atmosphere of the palace. And again and again, with developing conviction, he insisted that being born a mutation was something different and special and important. Anybody could be born an ordinary human, but few were chosen by the gods of the atoms.

There was danger, Joquin knew, in building up the ego of a Linn to feel superior even to the human members of his own family.

"But," as he explained one day to the Lord Leader, "he'll learn his limitations fast enough as he grows older. The important thing now is that his mind at the age of eight has become strong enough to withstand the most vulgar and sustained taunting from other boys. He still stammers and stutters like an idiot when he tries to talk back, and it's pitiful what happens to him when he is brought into contact with a new adult, but unless surprised, he has learned to control himself by remaining silent. I wish," Joquin finished, "that you would let him accustom himself to occasional visits from you."

It was an oft-repeated request, always refused. The refusals worried Joquin, who was nearly eighty years old. He had many anxious moments as to what would happen to the boy after his own death. And in order to insure that the blow would not be disasterous, he set about enlisting the support of famous scholars, poets and historians. These he first partially persuaded by argument, then introduced one by one as paid tutors to the boy. He watched each man with an alertness that swiftly eliminated those who showed in any way that they did not appreciate the importance of what was being attempted.

The boy's education turned out to be an expensive generosity, as neither the allowances of the Lord Leader, his grandfather, or of Lord Creg, his father, were sufficient to cover the fees of the many famous men Joquin employed. Indeed, when Joquin died, just before Clane's eleventh birthday, the liquid assets of the estate barely sufficed to pay the minor bequests after death taxes were deducted.

He left ten million sesterces to be divided among juniors,

initiates and seniors of various temples. Five million sesterces he bequested to personal friends. Two million more went to certain historians and poets in order that they might complete books which they had begun, and finally there were five great grandnephews who each received a million sesterces.

That disposed almost entirely of the available cash. A bare five hundred thousand sesterces remained to keep the vast farms and buildings of the estate in operation until the next crop was harvested. Since these were left in their entirety, along with upward of a thousand slaves, to Clane, there was a short period when the new owner, all unknown to himself, was on the verge of bankruptcy.

The situation was reported to the Lord Leader, and he advanced a loan from his private purse to tide over the estate. He also took other steps. He learned that Joquin's slaves were disgruntled at the idea of belonging to a mutation. He sent his spies among them to find out who were the ringleaders, and then hanged the four chief troublemakers as examples. It also came to his ears that Joquin's great grandnephews, who had expected the estate, were making dark threats about what they would do to the "usurper." The Lord Leader promptly confiscated their shares of the inheritance, and sent all five of them to join Lord Creg's army which was on the point of launching a major invasion against Mars.

Having done so much, the old ruler proceeded to forget all about his grandson. And it was not until some two years later, when, seeing the boy one morning pass beneath the window of his study, he grew curious.

That very afternoon he set out for the rock aerie to have a look at the strangest youth who had ever been born into the Linn family.

6

He was puffing by the time he reached the foot of the rock. That startled him. "By the four atom gods," he thought, "I'm getting old." He was sixty-three, within two months of sixty-four.

The shock grew. *Sixty-four*. He looked down at his long body. An old man's legs, he thought, not so old as some men of sixty-four, but there was no question any more that he was past his prime. "Creg was right," he thought, aghast. "The time has come for me at least to retrench. No more wars after Mars except defensive ones. And I must name Creg my heir and co-Lord Leader." It was too big a subject for the moment. The thought, heir, reminded him where he was. One of his grandsons was up there with a tutor. He could hear the murmuring baritone of the man, the occasional remark of the boy. It sounded very human and normal.

The Lord Leader frowned, thinking of the vastness of the world and the smallness of the Linn family. Standing there, he realized why he had come to this spot. Everyone of them would be needed to hold the government together. Even the lamebrains, even the mutations, must be given duties consonant with their abilities. It was a sad and terrible thing to realize that he was approaching the ever more lonely peak of his life, able to trust only those of his own blood. And even they clung together only because of the restless tide of ambition that surged on every side.

The old man smiled, a mixture of wry, grim humor. Something of the steely quality of him showed in the natural shape his jaws and chin assumed. It was the look of the man who had won the bloody battle of Attium that made Linn his; the smile of the man who had watched his soldiers hack Raheinl to pieces with battle-axes. "There was a man," he thought, still amazed after nearly thirty years, that the leader of the opposing group should have been so perverse. "What made him refuse all my offers? It was the first time in the history of civil war that such an attempt at conciliation was made. I was the compromiser. He wanted the world, and I did not want it, at least not in that way, but had to take it perforce to save my life. Why must men have all or nothing?"

Surely, Raheinl, cold and calm, waiting for the first axe to strike, must have realized the vanity of his purposes. Must have known, also, that nothing could save him; that soldiers who had fought and bled and feared for their lives would stand for no mercy to be shown their main enemy. In spite of the impossibility, Raheinl had received a measure of mercy. The Leader recalled with crystallike clarity his selection of the executioners. He had ordered that the very first blow be fatal. The crowd wanted a torture, a spectacle. They *seemed* to get it, but actually, it was a dead man who was hacked to bits before their eyes.

Watching the great Raheinl being destroyed chilled forever the soul of the Lord Leader. He had never felt himself a participant of the murder. The crowd was the killer. The crowd and its mindless emotions, its strength of numbers that no man could ignore without the deadliest danger to himself and his family. The crowd and its simple bloodthirstiness frightened him even while he despised it, and influenced him while he skilfully used it for his own ends. It was rather dreadful to think that not once in his entire life had he made a move that was not motivated by some consideration of the crowd.

He had been born into a world already devastated by two powerful opposing groups. Nor was it a question of which group one joined. When the opposition was in power they tried to kill, disgrace or exile all the members of every family of the other party. During such periods, the children

42

of many noble families were dragged through the streets on the ends of hooks and tossed into the river. Later, if you were among those who survived, it was a question of striving to attain power and some control of your own group. For that, also, could not be left to chance and sympathy. There were groups within groups, assassination to eliminate dangerous contenders for leadership. An enormous capacity on everybody's part for murder and treachery.

The survivors of that intricate battle of survival were—
tough.

The Lord Leader Linn pulled his mind slowly out of its depth of memory and began to climb the steps cut into the towering rock itself. The top of the rock had a length of twenty feet, and it was almost as wide. Joquin's slaves had deposited piles of fertile soil upon it, and from this soil flowering shrubs reared up gracefully, two of them to a height of nearly fifteen feet.

The mutation and the tutor sat in lawn chairs in the shade of the tallest shrub, and they were so seated that they were not immediately aware of the Lord Leader's presence.

"Very well, then," the scholar, Nellian, was saying, "we have agreed that the weakness of Mars is its water system. The various canals, which bring water down from the north pole, are the sole sources of water supply. It is no wonder that the Martians have set up temples in which they worship water as reverently as we worship the gods of the atoms. It is, of course, another matter," Nellian continued, "to know what use can be made of this weakness of Mars. The canals are so wide and so deep that they cannot, for instance, be poisoned even temporarily."

"Macrocosmically speaking," said the boy, "that is true. The molecular world offers few possibilities except the forces which man's own body can bring to bear."

The Lord Leader blinked. Had he heard correctly? Had he heard a boy of thirteen talk like *that?* He had been about to step forward and reveal himself. Now, he waited, startled and interested.

Clane continued, "The trouble with my father is that he

43

is too trusting. Why he should assume that it is bad luck which is frustrating his war, I don't know. If I were he I would examine the possibilities of treachery a little more carefully, and I'd look very close indeed at my inner circle of advisers."

Nellian smiled. "You speak with the positivity of youth. If you ever get onto a battlefield you will realize that no mental preconception can match the reality. Vague theories have a habit of collapsing in the face of showers of arrows and spears, and in-fighting with swords and axes."

The boy was imperturbable. "They failed to draw the proper conclusions from the way the spaceships carrying the water exploded. Joquin would have known what to think about that."

The talk, while still on a high grammatical level, was, it seemed to the Lord Leader, becoming a little childish. He stepped forward and cleared his throat.

At the sound, the scholar turned serenely, and then, as he saw who it was, he stood up with dignity. The mutation's reaction was actually faster, though there was not so much movement in it. At the first sound, he turned his head. And that was all. For a long moment, he sat frozen in that position. At first his expression remained unchanged from the quiet calm that had been on it. The Lord Leader had time for a close look at a grandson whom he had not seen so near since the day Clane was born.

The boy's head was human. It had the distinctive and finely shaped Linn nose and the Linn blue eyes. But it had something more, too. His mother's delicate beauty was somehow interwoven into the face. Her mouth was there, her ears and her chin. The face and head were beautifully human, almost angelic in their structure. It was not the only human part of him. But most of the rest was at very least subtly unhuman. The general shape was very, very man-like. The body, the torso, the legs and arms—they were all there, but wrong in an odd fashion.

The thought came to the Lord Leader that if the boy would wear a well-padded scholar's or scientist's gown, and keep his arms withdrawn into the folds—his hands were normal—no one would ever more than guess the truth. There was not even any reason why that face should not be put on one of the larger silver or gold coins, and circulated among certain remote and highly moral tribes. The angel qualities of Clane's face might very well warm many a barbarian heart.

"Thank the gods," thought the Lord Leader, not for the first time, "that he hasn't got four arms and four legs."

His mind reached that thought just as the paralysis left the boy. (It was only then that the Lord Leader realized that Clane had almost literally been frozen where he was.) Now, the transformation was an amazing spectacle. The perfect face began to change, to twist. The eyes grew fixed and staring, the mouth twitched and lost its shape. The whole countenance collapsed into a kind of idiocy that was terrible to see. Slowly, though it didn't take too long, the boy's body swung out of the chair, and he stood half crouching, facing his grandfather. He began to whimper, then to gibber.

Beside him, Nellian said sharply, "Clane, control yourself." The words were like a cue. With a low cry, the boy darted forward, and ducked past the Lord Leader. As he came to the steep stone stairway, he flung himself down it at a reckless speed, almost sliding down to the ground more than twenty feet below. Then he was gone down the pathway.

There was silence, and Nellian said finally, quietly, "May I speak?"

The Lord Leader noted that the scholar did not address him by his titles, and a fleeting smile touched his lips. An anti-imperialist. After a moment he felt annoyed—these upright republicans—but he merely nodded an affirmative to the verbal request.

Nellian said, "He was like that with me, also, when Joquin first brought me up to be his tutor. It is a reversion to an emotional condition which he experienced as a very young child."

The Lord Leader said nothing. He was gazing out over

the city. It was a misty day, so the haze of distance hid the farther suburbs. From this height, they seemed to melt into the haze—houses, buildings, land grown insubstantial. And yet, beyond, he could see the winding river, and the country-side partially hidden by the veils of mist. In the near distance were the circus pits, empty now that a great war was taxing the human resources of an Earth which had attained the colossal population of sixty million inhabitants. In his own lifetime, the number of people had nearly doubled.

It was all rather tremendous and wonderful, as if the race were straining at some invisible leash, with its collective eyes on a dazzling bright future, the realities of which were still hidden beyond remote horizons.

The Lord Leader drew his mind and his eyes back to the rock. He did not look directly at Nellian as he asked, "What did he mean when he said that my son, Lord Creg, should watch out for treachery close to him?"

Nellian shrugged. "So you heard that? I need hardly tell you that he would be in grave danger if certain ears heard that he had made such remarks. Frankly, I don't know where he obtains all his information. I do know that he seems to have a very thorough grasp of palace intrigue and politics. He's very secretive."

The Lord Leader frowned. He could understand the secretiveness. People who found out too much about other people's plans had a habit of turning up dead. If the mutation really knew that treachery had dogged the Martian war, even the hint of such knowledge would mean his assassination. The Leader hesitated. Then: "What did he mean about the spaceships with water blowing up just before they landed? What does he know about things like that?"

It was the other's turn to hesitate. Finally, Nellian said, "He's mentioned that several times. In spite of his caution, the boy is so eager for companionship, and so anxious to impress, that he keeps letting out his thoughts to people like myself whom he trusts."

The scholar looked steadily at the Lord Leader. "Naturally, I keep all such information to myself. I belong to no side politically."

The great man bowed ever so slightly. "I am grateful," he said, with a sigh.

Nellian said, after an interval, "He has referred a number of times to the Raheinl temple incident which occurred at the time of his birth, when four temples exploded. I have gathered that Joquin told him something about that, and also that Joquin left secret papers at his estate, to which the boy has had access. You may recall that he has visited the main estate three times since Joquin's death."

The Lord Leader recalled vaguely that his permission had been asked by Nellian on several occasions.

"I hope it is unnecessary for me to say," Nellian continued, "that the boy's mentality, as distinct from his emotional nature, is very mature, at least that of a nineteen-year-old."

"Hm-m-m," said the Lord Leader. His manner grew decisive. "We must cure him of his weakness. There are several methods." He smiled reminiscently. "In war, when we want to end a man's fear, we subject him to repeated dangers in actual combat. He might be killed, of course, but if he survives he gradually acquires confidence and courage. Similarly, an orator must first be trained in voice control, then he must speak again and again to acquire poise and an easy address."

The Leader's lips tightened thoughtfully. "We can hardly initiate him into war. The soldiers unfortunately regard mutations as ill omens. Public speaking—that can now best be done by putting him in one of the remoter temples. From the security of a scientist's robes, he can deliver the daily incantations, first to the atom gods in private, then in the presence of scientists, initiates and juniors and finally before the public. I will make arrangements for that experience to begin tomorrow. He does not need to live at the temple. Finally, sometime next year, we will assign him a separate residence, and secure for him a number of attractive slave girls. I want small, mild, meek girls, who will not try to

47

boss him. I'll select them myself, and give them a good talking to."

He added matter-of-factly, "They can be sold later in remote regions."

The Lord Leader paused, and looked keenly at Nellian. "What do you think of that as a beginning?"

The scholar nodded judicially. "Excellent, excellent. I I am glad to see you taking a personal interest in the boy."

The Lord Leader was pleased. "Keep me in touch about" —he frowned—"once every three months."

He was turning away when his gaze lighted on something half hidden in the brush at one edge of the rock. "What's that?" he asked.

Nellian looked embarrassed. "Why," he said, "why, uh, that's, uh, a device Joquin rigged up."

The scholar's self-consciousness amazed the Leader. He walked over and looked at the thing. It was a metal pipe that disappeared down the side of the rock. It was almost completely hidden by creeping vines, but little glints of it were visible here and there both against the rock and against the cliff farther down.

He drew back and was examining the open end of the pipe again, when it spoke huskily, a woman's voice: "Kiss me, kiss me again."

The Lord Leader placed a tuft of grass over the pipe end, and climbed to his feet, amused. "Well, I'll be a—" he said. "A listening device, straight down into one of the rendezvous spots of the palace grounds."

Nellian said, "There's another one on the other side."

The Lord Leader was about to turn away again, when he noticed the notebook beside the tube. He picked it up, and rippled through it. All the pages were blank, and that was puzzling until he saw the bottle of ink and the pen half hidden in the grass where the book had been.

He was genuinely interested now. He picked up the bottle, and pulled out the cork. First he looked hard at the ink, then he smelled it. Finally, with a smile, he reinserted the cork, and replaced the bottle on the grass.

As he descended the pathway, he was thinking, "Joquin was right. These mutations can be normal, even super-normal."

7

At this time, the Martian war was two years old, and it was already proving itself to be the most costly campaign ever launched. From the very beginning, when it was still in the planning stages, it had aroused men to bitter passions. To fight it or not to fight it—three years before that had been the question that split the inner government group into two violently opposing camps. Lord Creg Linn, father of Clane, son of the Lord Leader, and General-in-Chief of the expedition, was from the first completely and without qualification opposed to the war.

He had arrived at the city from Venus some three years before in his personal space yacht, and accompanied by most of his staff. He spent months, then, arguing with his family and with various powerful patrons.

"The time has come," he told his hearers, "for the empire to stand firm on all its frontiers. From a single city-state we have grown until we now dominate all Earth with the exception of a few mountainous territories. Four of the eleven island continents of Venus are allied to us. And we need not worry about the habitable moons of Jupiter, since they are inhabited by barbarians. The Martians, it is true, continue to rule their planet in a brutal fashion, but it would be wise to leave them alone. The tribes they have conquered are constantly rebelling against them, and will keep them busy for a measurable time. Accordingly, they are no danger

49

to us, and that must be our sole consideration for all future wars."

If reports were true, many patrons and knights were convinced by this reasoning. But when they saw that the Lord Leader favored the war, they quickly changed their minds, at least publicly.

The Lord Leader's wife, Lydia, and Lord Tews—Lydia's son by a previous marriage—were particularly in favor of the invasion. Their argument, which eventually became that of the Lord Leader, was that the Martians had condemned themselves to war by their complete refusal to have commercial and other intercourse with the rest of the solar system. Who knew what plans were being made, what armies were under secret training, or how many spaceships were building on a planet that for more than a dozen years had admitted no visitors.

It was a telling argument. Lord Creg's dry suggestion that perhaps the method used by the empire to invade the Venusian island of Cimbri was responsible, did not confound the supporters of the war. The method had been simple and deadly. The Cimbri, a suspicious tribe, agreed finally to permit visitors. They were uneasy when over a period of several months some thirty thousand stalwart young male visitors arrived singly and in groups. Their uneasiness was justified. One night the visitors assembled in the three major Cimbrin cities, and attacked all centers of control. By morning a hundred thousand inhabitants had been slain, and the island was conquered.

The commanding general of that expedition was Lord Tews. At his mother's insistence, an ashamed patronate voted him a triumph.

It was natural that the Lydia-Tews group should regard Creg's remark as a product of envy. The suggestion was made that his words were unworthy of so illustrious a man. More slyly, it was pointed out that his own wars had been drawn out, and that this indicated a cautious nature. Some even went so far as to say that he did not trust the fighting abilities of Linnan armies, and they immediately added the

50

comment that this was a base reflection on the military, and that the only real conclusion to be drawn was that he was personally a coward.

To Lord Creg, doggedly holding to his opinions, the greatest shock came when he discovered that his own wife, Tania, supported the opposition. He was so angry that he promptly sent her a bill of divorcement. The Lady Tania, whose only purpose in supporting the war was that it would enhance her husband's career, and accordingly improve her position, promptly suffered a nervous breakdown. A week later she was partially recovered, but her state of mind was clearly shown by the fact that she took a gig to her husband's headquarters in the camp outside the city. And, during the dinner hour, before hundreds of high officers, she crept to him on her hands and knees and begged him to take her back. The astounded Creg led her quickly through a nearby door, and they were reconciled.

From this time dated the change in the Lady Tania. Her arrogance was gone. She withdrew to a considerable extent from social activities, and began to devote herself to her home. Her proud, almost dazzling beauty deteriorated to stately good looks.

It was an anxious wife who kissed her husband good-by on an early spring day, and watched his spear-nosed yacht streak off to join the vast fleet of spaceships mobilizing on the other side of Earth for the take-off to Mars.

Spaceships, like all the instruments, weapons and engines of transport and war known since legendary times, had their limitations. They were the fastest thing possessed by man, but just how fast, no one had ever been able to decide. At the time of the invasion of Mars, the prevailing belief was that spaceships attained the tremendous speed of a thousand miles an hour in airless space. Since the voyage to Mars required from forty to a hundred days—depending upon the respective positions of the two planets—the distance of Mars at its nearest was estimated at one million miles.

It was felt by thousands of intelligent people that this figure must be wrong. Because, if it were correct, then some of the remoter stars would be hundreds of millions of miles away. This was so obviously ridiculous that it was frankly stated by many that the uncertainty reflected on the ability and learning of the temple scientists.

A spaceship one hundred and fifty feet long could carry two hundred men and no more on a trip to Mars lasting sixty days. It had room for many more, but the air supply created an insurmountable limitation. The air could be purified by certain chemicals for so long, then it gave out.

Two hundred men per ship—that was the number carried by each transport of the first fleet to leave Earth. Altogether there were five hundred ships. Their destination was the great desert known as Mare Cimmerium. A mile-wide canal cut through the edge of this desert, and for a hundred miles on either side of the canal the desert was forced back by green vegetation that fed on the thousands of tiny tributary canals. Oslin, one of the five important cities of the Martians was located in a great valley at a point where the canal curved like a winding river.

In a sense, the canals were rivers. During spring, the water in them flowed steadily from north to south, gradually slowing until, by mid-summer, there was no movement. Oslin had a population which was reported to be well over a million. Its capture would simultaneously constitute a devastating blow to the Martians and an unmatched prize for the conquerors.

The fleet reached Mars on schedule, all except one ship turning up at the rendezvous within the prescribed forty-eight hours. At midnight on the second day, the vessels proceeded ten abreast towards the canal and the city. A site some five miles from the city's outskirts had been selected, and, one after another, the lines of ships settled among the brush and on the open fields. They began immediately to discharge their cargoes—all the soldiers, most of the horses and enough equipment and food for a considerable period.

It was a dangerous six hours. Spaceships unloading were notoriously vulnerable to certain types of attack ships fitted with long metal rams, capable of piercing the thin metal plates of which the outer walls were constructed. For an attack ship to catch a transport in the air meant almost certain death for everyone aboard. The attacker, approaching from the side, transfixed an upper plate, and forced the transport over on its back. Since there were no drive tubes on the top-side to hold the ship in the air, it usually fell like a stone. Periodic attempts to install drive tubes on the top as well as on the bottom caused radioactive burns to crews and passengers, and no amount of interposed lead seemed to stop the interflow between the tubes.

The six hours passed without an attack. About two hours after dawn, the army began to move along the canal towards the city. When they had marched about an hour, the advance guards topped a hill overlooking a great valley beyond which was glittering Oslin. They stopped, rearing their horses. Then they began to mill around. Swiftly, a messenger raced back to Lord Creg, reporting an incredible fact. A Martian army was encamped in the valley, an army so vast that its tents and buildings merged into the haze of distance.

The general galloped forward to have a look. Those about him reported that he was never calmer as he gazed out over the valley. But his hopes for a quick, easy victory must have faded at that moment. The army ahead was the main Martian force, comprising some six hundred thousand men. It was under the personal command of King Winatgin.

Lord Creg had already made up his mind to attack at once, when a small fleet of enemy attack ships whisked over the hill, and discharged a shower of arrows at the group on the hill, wounding nearly four dozen soldiers. The General-in-Chief was unhurt, but the escape was too narrow for comfort. Swiftly, he gave the necessary orders.

His purpose was simple. King Winatgin and his staff undoubtedly knew now that an attack was coming. But it was one thing for him to have the information, and quite another to transmit it to an encamped and spread-out army. That was the only reason why the battle was ever in doubt.

The attackers were outnumbered six to one. The defense was stolid and uncertain at first, then it grew heavy from sheer weight of numbers. It was later learned that a hundred thousand Martians were killed or wounded, but the small Linnan army lost thirty thousand men, killed, prisoner and missing. And when it had still made no headway by late afternoon Lord Creg ordered a fighting retreat.

His troubles were far from over. As his troops fell back alongside the greenish red waters of the canal, a force of five thousand cavalry, which had been out on distant maneuvers, fell upon their rear, cutting them off from their camp, and turning their retreat away from the canal, towards the desert.

The coming of darkness saved the army from further destruction. They marched until after midnight, before finally sinking down into a fatigued sleep. There was no immediate rest for Lord Creg. He flashed fire messages to his ships waiting out in space. A hundred of them nosed cautiously down and discharged more equipment and rations. It was expected that attack ships would make sneak attacks on them, but nothing happened, and they effected a successful withdrawal before dawn. All too swiftly, the protecting darkness yielded to bright daylight.

The new materiel saved them that day. The enemy pressed at them hour after hour, but it was clear to Lord Creg that King Winatgin was not using his forces to the best advantage. Their efforts were clumsy and heavy-handed. They were easily outmaneuvered and towards evening, by leaving a cavalry screen to hold up the Martian army, he was able to break contact completely.

That night the Linnan army had a much needed rest, and Lord Creg's hopes came back. He realized that, if necessary, he could probably re-embark his forces and get off the planet without further losses. It was a tempting prospect. It fitted in with his private conviction that a war so ill begun had little chance of success.

But, reluctantly, he realized that return to Linn was out of the question. The city would consider that he had disgraced himself as a general. After all, *he* had selected the point of attack, even though he had disapproved of the campaign as a whole. And that was another thing. It might be assumed that he who had opposed the war, had deliberately lost the battle. No, definitely, he couldn't return to Linn. Besides, in any event he had to wait until the second fleet with another hundred thousand men aboard arrived about two weeks hence.

Two weeks? On the fourth day, the thin strip-like ditches of canal water began to peter out. By evening the soldiers were fighting on sand that shifted under their feet. Ahead, as far as the eye could see was a uniformly flat red desert. There was another canal out there somewhere about nineteen days march due east, but Lord Creg had no idea of taking his army on such a dangerous journey. Seventy thousand men would need a lot of water.

It was the first time in Creg's military career that he had ever been cut off from a water supply. The problem grew tremendous when eleven out of a dozen spaceships sent for water exploded as they approached the camp, and deluged the desert and the unlucky men immediately below with boiling water. One ship got through, but the water aboard was beginning to boil, and the ship was saved only when those aboard operated the airlock mechanism, letting the steaming water pour out onto the sand.

The almost cooked commander emerged shakily from the control room, and reported to Lord Creg. "We did as you ordered, sir. Got rid of all our equipment, and dunked the entire ship in the canal, using it as a tanker. It began to get hot immediately."

He cursed. "It's those blasted water gods that these Martians worship. They must have done it."

"Nonsense!" said Lord Creg. And ordered the man escorted back to his ship by four high officers.

It was a futile precaution. Other soldiers had the same idea. The water and canal gods of the Martians had started the water boiling, and so the ships had exploded. Lord Creg in a rough and ready speech delivered to a number of legions pointed out that nothing happened to water brought in the ordinary water tanks of the ships.

A voice interrupted him, "Why don't you bring the water in them then?"

The men cheered the remark, and it was scarcely an acceptable explanation after that to answer that the main body of ships could not be risked in such an enterprise.

On the seventh day the army began to get thirsty. The realization came to Lord Creg that he could not afford to wait for the arrival of the second fleet. He accordingly decided on a plan, which had been in the back of his mind when he originally selected Oslin as the city which his forces would attack.

That night he called down two hundred ships, and packed his army into them, nearly three hundred and fifty men to a ship. He assumed that Martian spies had donned the uniforms of dead Linnans, and were circulating around his camp. And so he did not inform his staff of the destination until an hour before the ships were due.

His plan was based on an observation he had made when, as a young man, he had visited Mars. During the course of a journey down the Oslin canal, he noticed a town named Magga. This town, set among the roughest and craggiest hills on Mars, was approachable by land through only four passes, all easily defendable. It had had a garrison twenty years before. But Lord Creg assumed rightly that, unless it had been reinforced since then, his men could overwhelm it. There was another factor in his favor, though he did not know it at the time of his decision. King Winatgin, in spite of certain private information, could scarcely believe that the main Linnan invasion was already defeated. Hourly expecting vast forces to land, he kept his own armies close to Oslin.

Magga was taken shortly after midnight. By morning the troops were ready for siege with a plentiful supply of water. When the second fleet arrived a week later, they too settled in Magga, and the expedition was saved.

The extent of this defensive victory was never fully appreciated in Linn, not even by Lord Creg's followers and apologists. All that the people could see was that the army was jammed into a small canal town, and seemed doomed, surrounded as it was by a force which outnumbered it more than six to one. Even the Lord Leader, who had taken many a seemingly impregnable position in his military days, secretly questioned his son's statement that they were safe.

Except for forays, the army remained all that summer and the following winter in Magga. It was besieged the whole of the next year, while Lord Creg doggedly demanded another two hundred thousand men from a patronate which was reluctant to send more men into what they considered certain destruction. Finally, however, the Lord Leader realized that Creg was holding his own, and personally demanded the reinforcements. Four new legions were on their way on the day that the Lord Leader descended the pathway that led down from the aerie-sanctuary of his mutation grandson.

8

The Lord Leader was not greatly surprised two weeks later when Nellian handed him a message from Clane. The letter read:

To my grandfather,
Most Honorable Lord Leader:

I regret exceedingly that my emotions were so uncontrollable when you came to see me. Please let me say that I am proud of the honor you have done me, and that your visit has changed my mind about many things. Before you came to the aerie, I was not prepared to think of myself as having any obligations to the Linn family. Now, I have decided to live up to the name, which you have made illustrious. I salute you, honorable grandfather, the greatest man who ever lived.

Your admiring and humble grandson
Clane

It was, in its way, a melodramatic note, and the Lord Leader quite seriously disagreed with the reference to himself as the greatest man of all time. He was not even the second, though perhaps the third.

"My boy," he thought, "you have forgotten *my* uncle, the general of generals, and his opponent the dazzling personality who was given a triumph before he was twenty, and officially when he was still a young man voted the right to use the word 'great' after his name. I knew them both, and I *know* where I stand."

Nevertheless, in spite of its wordy praise, the letter pleased the Lord Leader. But it puzzled him, too. There were overtones in it, as if a concrete decision had been made by somebody who had the power to do things.

He put the letter among his files of family correspondence, starting a new case labeled "CLANE." Then he forgot about it. It was recalled to his mind a week later when his wife showed him two missives, one a note addressed to herself, the second an unsealed letter to Lord Creg on Mars. Both the note and the letter were from Clane. The stately Lydia was amused.

"Here's something that will interest you," she said.

The Lord Leader read first the note addressed to her. It was quite a humble affair.

To my most gracious grandmother,
Honorable lady:

Rather than burden your husband, my grandfather, with my request, I ask you most sincerely to have the enclosed letter sent by the regular dispatch pouch to my father, Lord Creg. As you will see it is a prayer which I shall make at the temple next week for his victory over the

Martians this summer. A metal capsule, touched by the god-metals, Radium, Uranium, Plutonium and Ecks, will be dedicated at this ceremony, and sent to my father on the next mail transport.

Most respectfully yours,
Clane

"You know," said Lydia, "for a moment when I received that, I didn't even know who Clane was. I had some vague idea that he was dead. Instead, he seems to be growing up."

"Yes," said the Lord Leader absently, "yes, he's growing."

He was examining the prayer which Clane had addressed to Lord Creg. He had an odd feeling that there was something here which he was not quite grasping. Why had this been sent through Lydia? Why not direct to himself?

"It's obvious," said Lady Linn, "that since there is to be a temple dedication, the letter must be sent."

That was exactly it, the Lord Leader realized. There was nothing here that was being left to chance. They *had* to send the letter. They *had* to send the metal dedicated to the gods.

But why was the information being conveyed through Lydia? He reread the prayer, fascinated this time by its ordinariness. It was so trite, so unimportant, the kind of prayer that made old soldiers wonder what they were fighting for—morons? The lines were widely spaced, to an exaggerated extent, and it was that, that suddenly made the Leader's eyes narrow ever so slightly.

"Well," he laughed, "I'll take this, and have it placed in the dispatch pouch."

As soon as he reached his apartment, he lit a candle, and held the letter over the flame. In two minutes, the invisible ink was beginning to show in the blank space between the lines. Six lines of closely written words between each line of the prayer. The Lord Leader read the long, precise instructions and explanations, his lips tight. It was a plan of attack for the armies on Mars, not so much military as magical. There were several oblique references to the blowing up of the temples many years before, and a very tremendous implication that something entirely different could be counted on from the gods.

At the end of the letter was a space for *him* to sign. He did not sign immediately, but in the end he slashed his signature on to the sheet, put it into the envelope and affixed his great seal of state. Then he sat back, and once more the thought came: *But why Lydia?*

Actually, it didn't take long to figure out the extent of the treachery that had baffled Lord Creg's sorely pressed legions for three years.

As close as that, the Lord Leader thought grayly. As close in the family as that. Some of the plotting must have been done in one or the other of the rendezvous some sixty feet below the rock aerie where a child of the gods lay with his ear pressed to a metal tube listening to conspiratorial words, and noting them down in invisible ink on the pages of an apparently blank notebook.

The Lord Leader was not unaware that his wife intrigued endlessly behind his back. He had married her, so that the opposition would have a skilful spokesman in the government. She was the daughter of one of the noblest families in Linn, all the adult males of which had died fighting for Raheinl. Two of them were actually captured and executed. At nineteen, when she was already married and with child— later born Lord Tews— the Lord Leader arranged with her husband for what was easily the most scandalous divorce and remarriage in the history of Linn. The Lord Leader was unconcerned. He had already usurped the name of the city and empire Linn for his family. The next step was to make a move to heal what everybody said was the unhealable wound left by the civil war. Marriage to Lydia was that move, and a wondrously wise one it had been.

She was the safety valve for all the pent-up explosive forces of the opposition. Through her maneuvers, he learned what they were after. And gave as much as would satisfy. By seeming to follow her advice, he brought hundreds of able administrators, soldiers and patrons from the other side into the government service to manage the unwieldy populations of Earth, and rule solar colonies. In the previous ten years, more and more opposition patrons had supported his laws in the patronate without qualification. They laughed a little at the fact that he still read all his main speeches. They ridiculed his stock phrases: "Quicker than you can cook asparagus." "Words fail me, gentlemen." "Let's be satisfied with the cat we have." And others. But again and again during the past decade, all party lines dissolved in the interests of the empire. And, when his agents reported conspiracies in the making, further investigation revealed that no powerful men or families were involved.

Not once had he blamed Lydia for the various things she had done. She could no more help being of the opposition than he, years before, had been able to prevent himself from being drawn, first as a youth, then as a man, into the vortex of the political ambitions of his own group. She would have been assassinated if it had ever seemed to the more hotheaded of the opposition that she was "betraying" them by being too neutral.

No, he didn't blame her for past actions. But this was different. Vast armies had been decimated by treachery, so that Lord Creg's qualities as a leader would show up poorly in comparison to Lord Tews'. This was personal, and the Lord Leader recognized it immediately as a major crisis. The important thing, he reasoned, was to save Creg, who was about to launch his campaign. But meanwhile, great care must be taken not to alarm Lydia and the others. Undoubtedly, they must have some method of intercepting his private mail pouch to Creg. Dared he stop that? It wouldn't be wise to do so.

Everything must appear normal and ordinary, or their fright might cause some foolhardy individual to attempt an impromptu assassination of the Lord Leader. As it was, so long as Lord Creg's armies were virtually intact, the group would make no radical moves.

The pouch, with Clane's letter in it, would have to be allowed to fall into their hands, as other pouches must have done. If the letter were opened, an attempt would probably be made to murder Clane. Therefore—what?

The Lord Leader placed guards in every rendezvous of the palace grounds, including two each in the two areas at the foot of the aerie. His posted reason for setting the guards was on all the bulletin boards:

I am tired of running into couples engaged in licentious kissing. This is not only in bad taste, but it has become such a common practice as to require drastic action. The guards will be removed in a week or so. I am counting on the good sense of everyone, particularly of the women, to see to it that in future these spectacles are voluntarily restricted.

A week or so to protect Clane until the dedication at the temple.

It would be interesting to see just what the boy did do with the dedicated metal, but, of course, his own presence was impossible. It was the day after the dedication that the Lord Leader spoke to Nellian. "I think he should make a tour of Earth," he said. "Haphazard, without any particular route. And incognito. And start soon. Tomorrow."

So much for Clane. More personal, he made a friendly visit to the guard's camp outside the city. For the soldiers, it turned out to be an unexpectedly exciting day. He gave away a million sesterces in small but lavish amounts. Horse races, foot races and contests of every kind were conducted, with prizes for the winners; and even losers who had tried nobly were amazed and delighted to receive money awards.

All in all, it was a satisfactory day. When he left, he heard cheers until he reached the Martian gate. It would take several weeks at least, if not months, to cause disaffection among those troops.

The various precautions taken, the Lord Leader dispatched the mail pouch, and awaited events.

Lydia's group had to work fast. A knight emptied the mail pouch. A knight and a patron scrutinized each letter, and separated them into two piles. One of these piles, the largest one by far, was returned to the pouch at once. The other pile was examined by Lord Tews, who extracted from it some score of letters, which he handed to his mother.

Lydia looked at them one by one, and handed those she wanted opened to one or the other of two slaves, who were skilled in the use of chemicals. It was these slaves who actually removed the seals.

The seventh letter she picked up was the one from Clane. Lydia looked at the handwriting on the envelope, and at the name of the sender on one side, and there was a faint smile on her lips. "Tell me," she said, "am I wrong, or does the army regard dwarfs, mutations and other human freaks as bad omens?"

"Very much so," said one of the knights. "To see one of them on the morning of battle spells disaster. To have any contact with one means a great setback."

The Lady Leader smiled. "My honorable husband is almost recalcitrantly uninterested in such psychological phenomena. We must accordingly see to it that Lord Creg's army is apprized that he has received a message from his mutation son."

She tossed the letter towards the pouch. "Put this in. I have already seen the contents."

Hardly more than three quarters of an hour later, the dispatch carrier was again on his way to the ship.

"Nothing important," Lydia said to her son. "Your stepfather seems to be primarily concerned these days with preserving the moral stature of the palace grounds."

Lord Tews said, thoughtfully, "I'd like to know why he felt it necessary to bribe the guards' legion the other day."

What was much more surprising to the conspirators occurred the following day, when the Lord Leader called the two chambers of the Patronate into joint session. As soon as possible after the announcement was made, the Lady Lydia attended upon her husband in his apartment, and questioned him about it. But the great man shook his head, and smiled, and said without apparent guile: "My dear, it will be a pleasant surprise for everyone. You must permit me a few simple pleasures of this kind."

By the time the special session began a few days later, her spies had still not found a clue to the subject matter to be dealt with. Both she and Lord Tews sought out, and talked to, some of the leaders of the Patronate in the hope that they would have, as Lydia put it, a "thimbleful of information." But it was clear to her, from the way that she herself was adroitly questioned, that they were as much in the dark as she. And so for the first time in many years, she had the unhappy experience of sitting in her box at the Patronate without knowing in advance what was scheduled to happen.

The fateful moment arrived. She watched her husband stride along the aisle and mount the podium, and in a final anguish of doubt and exasperation, she clutched the sleeve of Tews' jacket, and whispered fiercely: "What can he possibly have in mind? The whole affair has become fantastic."

Tews said nothing.

The Lord Leader, Medron Linn, began in the formal, prescribed fashion:

"Most excellent members of my family, gracious and astute leaders of the Patronate, noble Patrons and their worthy families, Knights of the Realm and their ladies, honorable members of the public house, representatives of the good people of the empire of Linn—it is with pleasure that I announce a decision which I feel sure will immediately have your support—"

That was chilling. There was a stir in the audience, and then a settling down. Lydia closed her eyes and quivered with frustration. Her husband's words meant that there would be no debate, and no discussion. The Patronate would later go through the form of ratification, but actually the announcement the Lord Leader was making would virtually become law as he spoke the words.

Tews leaned towards his mother. "Notice," he said, "he is not reading his speech."

Lydia had not noticed. She should have, she realized wanly. Her spies among the household attendants had reported often enough that they could find no discarded papers, no speeches half written, no scribblings anywhere in the Lord Leader's apartment or offices.

On the podium, Medron Linn continued:

"It is not easy for a man who has been as active as I have to realize that the years are creeping up. But there seems to be no doubt that I have grown older and that I am physically less robust today than I was ten years ago, or even ten months ago. The time has accordingly come for me to consider naming an heir, and by that I mean not only a successor but a joint administrator, who will be co-Lord Leader while I remain in office, and senior Lord Leader after my retirement or death. With these thoughts in mind, it is my great joy to inform you that I have selected for this important position my beloved son, Lord Creg, whose long and honorable public career has in the past few years been augmented by several major achievements."

One after another he listed successes of Lord Creg in his early career. Then:

"His first great achievement in the Martian campaign, so ill-begun, was when he rescued his army from the unfortunate coincidence which brought him into direct contact with greatly superior enemy forces at the moment of landing, and which could have resulted in an unparalleled disaster for Linnan arms. It is almost a miracle that he has again brought his army to the point where he can shortly take the offensive, but this time we can be sure that he will gain the victory which was snatched from him by accident two years ago."

He paused, and then while Lydia listened, with eyes open now, already resigned to the disaster that was here for her, he said firmly:

"Upon my son, Lord Creg, I now bestow joint administratorship with myself of the entire Linnan empire, and upon my son, Lord Creg, I bestow the title, Lord Leader. This title, though junior to mine, is not intended to be administratively inferior, except insofar as a son honors and respects his father."

The Lord Leader paused, and smiled a strange, bleak smile for his grim face, and went on:

"I know that you will enjoy these happy tidings with me, and that you will proceed rapidly—indeed, I suggest that this be the day and this the hour—with the legal forms of the appointment, so that we may advise my son of the honor given him by the empire on the eve of his decisive battle."

He bowed, and stepped down. It seemed to require a moment for the audience to realize that he was through, for there was silence. However, the clapping was all the more frenzied when it finally began, and it lasted until he was out of the great marble room.

9

Lord Creg read the letter from Clane with an amazed frown. He recognized that the boy's prayer had been used to convey a more important message, and the fact that such a ruse had been necessary startled him. It gave a weight to the document, which he would not ordinarily have attached to so wild a plan.

The important thing about it was that it required only slight changes in the disposition of his troops. His intention was to attack. It assumed that he would attack, and added a rather unbelievable psychological factor. Nevertheless, in its favor was the solid truth that eleven spaceships filled with water had exploded, a still unexplained phenomenon after two years.

Creg sat for a long time pondering the statement in the letter that the presence of King Winatgin's army at Oslin had not been an accident, but had been due to treachery hitherto unknown in Linn. "I've been cooped up here for two years," he thought bitterly, "forced to fight a defensive war because my stepmother and her plumpish son craved unlimited power."

He pictured himself dead, and Tews succeeding to the Lord Leadership. After a moment, that seemed appalling. Abruptly, decisively, he called on a temple scientist attached to the army, a man noted for his knowledge of Mars. "How fast do the Oslin canal waters move at this time of the year?"

"About five miles an hour," was the reply.

Creg considered that. About one hundred and thirty miles in a Martian day. A third of that should be sufficient, or even less. If the dedicated metal were dropped about twenty miles north of the city, the effect, whatever it was, would be achieved just as his long-planned attack was finally launched. It would certainly do no harm to include such a minor action as part of the assault preparation. So—even in his anger—he reassured himself.

The army was still preparing for the assault, when the news arrived from Earth that Creg had been appointed co-Lord Leader. The new joint ruler of the Linnan empire released the announcement in a modestly worded communique to all ranks—and was almost immediately amazed at the response. Wherever he went, men shouted the news of his coming, and there was wild cheering. He had previously been informed by his intelligence officers that his men appreciated the icy skill with which he had extricated them from the trap at the time of the original landing. But now he felt himself the object of warm personal regard.

In the past, he had occasionally observed the friendliness which some officers inspired in their men. For the first time, the comradely feeling was for him. It made all the years of hardship in the field, the strain of maintaining integrity amid so many corruptions, worthwhile. As a friend and as an adviser, as General-in-Chief and as a fellow man-at-arms, Lord Leader, Creg Linn, addressed his men in a special bulletin issued at dawn of the day of attack.

Soldiers of Linn—The day and the hour of victory are upon us. We have ample forces and an overwhelming abundance of arms to achieve every purpose which we desire. In these moments before the decisive battle is joined, let us remember once more that the goal of victory is a unified solar system, one people, and one universe. We are not concerned with the corruption which is sometimes attendant upon the achievement of great purposes. Our goal is an immediate and overwhelming success. But bear in mind, victory is always the result of unflinching determination combined with the skills of the veteran fighting man. I therefore admonish you—for your life and for victory, stand firmly wherever you are, move forward whenever you can. As soldiers, we dedicate ourselves with the truest and purest motives to the atom gods, and to victory. Each and every one of you has my personal best wishes.

Creg Linn,
Lord Leader

The second battle of Oslin was never in doubt. On the morning of the battle, the inhabitants of the city awoke to find the mile wide canal and all its tributary waters a seething mass of boiling, steaming water. The steam poured over the city in dense clouds. It hid the spaceships that plunged down into the streets. It hid the soldiers who debouched from the ships. By mid-morning King Winatgin's army was surrendering in such numbers that the royal family was unable to effect an escape. The monarch, sobbing in his dismay, requested the protection of a Linnan officer, who led him under escort to the co-Lord Leader. The defeated ruler flung himself at Creg's feet, and then, given mercy, but chained, stood on a hill beside his captor, and watched the collapse of the Martian military might.

In a week, all except one remote mountain stronghold had surrendered, and Mars was conquered. At the height of the triumph, about dusk one day, a poisoned arrow snapped out of the shadows of an Oslin building and pierced Lord

Creg's throat. He died an hour later in great pain, his murderer still unfound. When the news of his death reached Linn three months later, both sides worked swiftly. Lydia had executed the two slave chemists and the dispatch carrier a few hours after she heard of Creg's victory. Now, she sent assassins to murder the two knights and the patron who had assisted in the opening of the mail. And, simultaneously, she ordered Tews to leave the city for one of his estates.

By the time the old Lord Leader's guards arrived to arrest him, the alarmed young man was off on his private spaceship. It was that escape that took the first edge off the ruler's anger. He decided to postpone his visit to Lydia. Slowly, as that first day dragged by, a bleak admiration for his wife built up inside him, and he realized that he could not afford to jeopardize his relations with her, not now when the great Creg was dead. He decided that she had not actually ordered the assassination of Creg. Some frightened henchman on the scene, fearing for his own safety, had taken his own action; and Lydia, with a masterly understanding of the situation, had merely covered up for them all. It might be fatal to the empire if he broke with her now. By the time she came with her retinue to offer him official condolences, his mind was made up. He took her hand in his with tears in his eyes.

"Lydia," he said, "this is a terrible moment for me. What do you suggest?"

She suggested a combination State funeral and Triumph. She said, "Unfortunately, Tews is ill, and will not be able to attend. It appears to be an illness that may keep him away for a long time."

The Lord Leader recognized that it was a surrender of her ambition for Tews, at least for the time being. It was in reality a tremendous concession, not absolutely necessary in view of his own determination to keep the whole affair private.

He bent and kissed her hand. At the funeral, they marched together behind the coffin. And because his mind was uneasy with doubts about the future, he kept thinking: "What

69

now?" It was an agony of indecision, of awareness of the limitations of one aging man.

He was still thinking and wondering frantically, when his gaze lighted upon a boy wearing the mourning robes of a scientist. The youngster walked beside the scholar Nellian, and that brought recognition that it was his grandson, Clane.

The Lord Leader walked on behind the glittering coffin which contained the remains of his dead son, and now for the first time, some of the anguish faded from his set face, and he grew thoughtful. It was not as if he could build much hope on a mutation. And yet he recalled what Joquin had once said, about giving the boy a chance to grow up. "It will be up to him after that," the now-dead temple scientist had said. And he had gone on to predict that Clane "will carve his own niche in the Linnan hall of fame."

Medron Linn, a bereaved and desperate man, smiled grimly. The boy's training must go on, and for a change a little emotional development might be in order.

Although he was barely at puberty, it was probably time for Clane to discover that women were live bundles of emotion, dangerous yet delightful. Experience with women might well force a balance of mind and body, which an over-intellectualized existence had disturbed.

10

"The Deglet family, later renamed Linn," said the scholar, Nellian, to his pupil, Lord Clane Linn, "entered the commercial banking business in a very simple fashion about 150 years ago."

It was a warm summer day a few weeks after the funeral

of Lord Creg. The two sat under a large smoke tree in the inner grounds of the country estate which Clane had inherited from Joquin. The fourteen-year-old boy, instead of answering, partly raised himself from his seat. He gazed along the road which led to the city of Linn eighty miles away. A cloud of dust was visible on the horizon, and once —as he watched—sunlight glinted on metal. It could have been a turning wheel, but it was still too far distant for details to be identifiable.

Clane realized that fact abruptly, for he settled back in his chair, and his words, when he spoke, were a comment on what Nellian had said. Was it not true that the founder of the family sat on a street corner, and loaned money to passersby in return for keepsakes, such as jewels and rings?

"I do believe," nodded the old man, "that your ancestor was an astute money-lender, and knew his fine metals and precious rocks. But he did presently move into an establishment."

The boy chuckled. "A one-room wooden structure, very poorly protected from the weather."

"Still," said his tutor, "the greater dignity of 'quarters' was attained, and history tells us that, after he was able to purchase slaves, he built himself a series of structures of varying degrees of quality, making appointments for particular days at each one, and changing clothes to suit each establishment. Thus in the course of a week, he would meet a cross section of the population, one day loaning money from his wooden shack to a workman, and the following day, perhaps dealing on a vastly larger scale with a knightly family, who would borrow a small amount of cash on their valuable land and buildings, their purpose being to maintain a front which they could not of course afford. Your ancestor recognized the irrationality of such false pride, and with icy objectivity took advantage of it. Presently, he owned large homes and estates, and had enemies, who had foolishly signed over their property in return for a few months more in which to delude themselves." Nellian paused, and looked questioningly at his pupil. He said: "The look on your face suggests that what I'm saying has made you thoughtful, young man."

It had. But Clane was silent, shaking his head a little with the insights that were flashing through his mind. He said finally, "I'm thinking that pride has been the downfall of individuals and empires." It was more than that. He was remembering his own tendency to become paralyzed in the presence of certain individuals. Could it be that that was his way of maintaining his pride.

He explained the insight to Nellian. "As I see it, I can keep my self-esteem in such a situation if I pretend to myself that I am dominated by something inside me over which I have no control. Under such circumstances, I can feel self-pity, but do not have to lose face with myself."

He shook his head, and then—remembering—looked up, and stared into the distance over the uneven green hills, where the dust cloud now featured a continuous glint of sunlight on metal. He shook his head because it was still an unrecognizable mass, and said unhappily: "I wonder if I've done that so often that now I *cannot* control it."

"You're getting better all the time," said Nellian quickly.

"That's true." The boy nodded, and he was relieved because he had momentarily forgotten the fact of his development. "I'm like a soldier who becomes more of a veteran with each battle he survives." He frowned. "Unfortunately, there are certain wars I haven't fought yet."

Nellian smiled grimly. "You must continue to fight a series of limited engagements, as Joquin and you decided long ago. And—I believe, from a report which was conveyed to me recently—it is a policy with which your grandfather concurs."

Clane looked at him with narrowed eyes. "Why should my grandfather have considered such a matter—recently?"

The long, somewhat lined countenance of the tutor broke into a quizzical smile. "It's a legal situation," he said.

"Legal?"

"Your status," said Nellian gently, "was altered when your father was confirmed as co-Lord Leader."

72

"Oh, that!" Clane shrugged under the loose fitting temple gown he wore. "That has little practical meaning. As a mutation, I am like the hunchback of a family, who is tolerated because of the blood connection. When I grow up, I can act as an intriguer behind the scenes of power. At best I may play the role of a priestly liaison between the temples and the government. My future promises to be stereotyped and sterile."

"Nevertheless," said Nellian, "as one of the three sons of co-Lord Leader Creg Linn, you have legal rights within the government, which you will have to deal with whether you like it or not." He finished crustily: "And permit me to inform you, young man, if your attitude of negation reflects your true feelings, then both Joquin and I have wasted our time and effort. In the troubled State of Linn, you will either live up to your rank, or be dead at an assassin's hand before you attain your majority."

The boy said coldly: "Old man, continue with your history lesson."

Nellian smiled bleakly. "In a different manner, your prospects parallel those of your ancestor, whom we were discussing. You, the despised mutation. He, the despised money lender. Surely, you will recognize that the handicaps under which he labored were as great, or greater than, your own. And yet, my boy, we are talking about the man who founded the Linn family. Looking ahead for you, we see only difficulties. Looking back on his career, we can see how simple it all was for a bold man operating among irrational people. You see, a computable percentage of the better families who borrowed money from him did nothing with what they had loaned except maintain their pretense a little longer. And, of course, when ruin struck, they blamed, not themselves, but wily young Govan Deglet, who merely hired a few more personal guards, and foreclosed on their property. In his early thirties, he was already so wealthy that he could look around among the nearly ruined families of patrons and presently make a proposal of marriage which shocked the quality folk of that day to the cores of their aristocratic souls. But Patron Senner was a man who faced realities; and so, in order to save himself from disaster, he arranged the marriage contract whereby his beautiful daughter, Piccarda Senner, thereafter shared the bed of the famous money lender and bore his children—which, by the way, she resented all her life. She called them, including your great, great, great grandfather, her bondsman brats."

The thin face of the boy twisted into a cynical smile. "If she were that opposed," he said, "I cannot accept that the children were his. Remember, Nellian, up in my retreat at the palace, I have listened for years to the adulteries of the famous ladies of the Court, all respectably married, according to outward appearance, yet capable of one liaison after another. I never heard one who was not quite open about the possibility that the child each carried at any particular moment was possibly not of the husband. It is unimportant, of course, whether or not we Linns are direct descendants of Govan Deglet. We inherited his money, and the Senner connection brought family prestige to the children. But—" He shrugged.

Nellian was smiling. "Govan knew his aristocratic women and their morals. He had his wife watched at all times; and presently, being a woman of passion, she realized that her only resource was her husband. History records that he was a happy and satisfied man."

The scholar climbed to his feet. "Young man," he said, "I believe we should terminate this lesson. In a few minutes your grandfather, the Lord Leader, will be here—"

"My grandfather!" Clane was on his feet, trembling. All in a flash, the self-possession faded from him. He steadied himself with a terrible effort, and said: "What does he want?"

"He is bringing a couple of recently captured Martian girl slaves to be your mistresses. Very beautiful youngsters, I'm told."

He stopped. He had lost his audience.

For Clane, Nellian's words dissolved into meaningless sounds, and then—

Blankness!

74

Once, after that—it could have been that evening—he was aware of himself crouching on the floor of his bedroom, and there was a frightened girl peering at him from his bed. She was saying hysterically: "I won't. You can kill me. But he's not normal. I won't!"

The Lord Leader's voice came from somewhere out of Clane's line of vision, coldly: "Take her out and whip her. Four lashes. But don't damage her skin."

The next time Clane was aware, the girl was bending over him. "You poor creature. You're as badly off as I am, aren't you? Why not come into the bed? We have to go through with this."

The pity of her voice blanked him out. Pity, he couldn't stand from anyone.

He had a sense of the passage of time. And there were several fantasies of love making, which could have been real, but they didn't seem so. In those fantasies, he was violent and insatiable, the girl timid and tender.

Other fantasies came. Occasionally, they now included a second girl. Somewhere in there, he heard Nellian say: "It's amazing to me. I didn't know the male human body had so great a love potential."

And still, as the months rolled by, it was like a dream. He seemed to know that the name of the first girl was Selk. He never did learn the name of the second, or if there were others—their names—not even in fantasy.

Because, presently, he was rejecting all except Selk. It was at this point that he had his sharpest awareness. His grandfather was lecturing him; and one sentence of that lecture stayed with him through many days. The sentence was: "...My boy, if you insist that she be the only one, then you will have to adjust yourself to her abilities..."

Clane had the distinct impression of making an agreement within himself that the Lord Leader was right, and that he would adjust.

He came to, while he was eating with Nellian. He paused in the act of biting a piece of meat; and there must have been something in his manner, for the scholar paused also, and said after a moment: "Anything on your mind, Clane?"

The boy nodded: "I'd like us to continue what we were discussing the other day," he said, "about my ancestor, Govan—what of his children?"

Nellian sighed with relief, and mentally dictated a letter to the Lord Leader. "Your excellency," he indited silently, "after one year and eight months, Lord Clane seems to have recovered from the emotional disaster of being introduced to female companionship. The brain is indeed a strange instrument."

Aloud, he said: "Your great, great, great grandfather, Cosan Deglet, was a banker and a Patron. He had branches in all the principal cities. . . ."

The history of the Deglet-become-Linn family had another, more mature student. For seven years, after the assassination of Creg, Lord Tews lived on Awai in the great sea.

He had a small property on the largest island of the group, and, after his disgrace, his mother had suggested that he retire there rather than to one of his more sumptuous mainland estates. A shrewd, careful man, he recognized the value of the advice. His role, if he hoped to remain alive, must be sackcloth and ashes.

At first it was purposeful cunning. In Linn, Lydia racked her brain for explanations and finally came out with the statement that her son had wearied and sickened of politics, and retired to a life of meditation beyond the poisoned waters. For a long time, so plausible and convincing was her sighing, tired way of describing his feelings—as if she, too, longed for the surcease of rest from the duties of her position—that the story was actually believed.

Patrons, governors and ambassadors, flying out in spaceships from Linn to the continents across the ocean, paused as a matter of course to pay their respects to the son of Lydia. Gradually they began to realize that he was out of favor. Desperately, terribly, dangerously out of favor.

The stiff-faced silence of the Lord Leader when Tews was mentioned was reported finally among administrators and politicians everywhere. People were tremendously astute, once they realized. It was recalled that Tews had hastily departed from Linn at the time when the news of the death of General Lord Creg, son of the Lord Leader, was first brought from Mars. At the time his departure had scarcely been remarked. Now it was remembered and conclusions drawn. Great ships, carrying high government officials, ceased to stop, so that the officials could float down for lunch with Lord Tews.

The isolation affected Tews profoundly. He became tremendously observant. He noticed in amazement for the first time that the islanders swam in the ocean. In water that had been poisoned since legendary times by the atom gods. Was it possible the water was no longer deadly? He noted the point for possible future reference, and for the first time grew interested in the name the islanders had for the great ocean. Passfic. Continental people had moved inland to escape the fumes of the deadly seas, and they had forgotten the ancient names.

He speculated on the age of a civilization, that had suffered so great a disaster that—in withdrawing from the shores of the radiation-poisoned oceans—the very names of those bodies of water had been lost with the passing of time. How long? He could only guess: thousands of years.

He wrote his mother on one occasion: "As you know, this is not a subject which has much engaged my interest. But now, for the first time, I find myself troubled by speculations as to the origin of our culture. Is it possible that, instead of engaging in endless intrigue, we should be attempting to piece together the past, with a view to discovering the nature of the destructive forces that were long ago loosed upon this planet? What disturbs me is the fact that whoever acted against Earth seemed to be prepared virtually to destroy the planet. Such ruthlessness is a new idea for me, and although it is only a speculation, I find myself looking into the future with a sense of unease. Is it possible that the struggle among groups seeking power can lead to ever greater excesses, until finally the world itself is convulsed by their madness? I propose to look into such matters more closely, with a view to arriving at a sane philosophy of government."

In another letter, he declared: "It has always been a vexation to me that our weapons are so primitive. I have been inclined to accept the old fables that in the distant past fire weapons of various types existed. As you know, we have a very strange paradox in our culture. We have machines which are so carefully constructed that they can be sealed against air loss in journeys through interplanetary space. The knowledge about metals, which makes this possible, is a heritage of Linn, which no one has ever been able to trace to the original creators. On the other hand, our weapons are bows and arrows, and spears. My tendency at the moment is to speculate that what followed such primitive devices in the olden days was superseded by entirely new types of weapons, which in their turn may also have been superseded. This would mean that the intermediate weapons simply vanished from the culture; the art of making them was lost. These ultimate devices were evidently much more difficult to manufacture—I am still speculating—and so the art could not just be handed down from father to son, as has happened with metallurgical knowledge. We know that, even in barbarous times, the temples were repositories of manufacturing knowledge, and it might almost seem as if someone deliberately set them up with a view to safeguarding ancient knowledge. We also know that, from a very early time the temples set themselves against warlike activity, and so it is possible that they deliberately destroyed information having to do with the production of weapons."

Among other things, Tews made his most careful study of the rise of the Linn family, from its Deglet origin. Even as Clane studied the same history, Tews noted that Cosan Deglet, son of the family founder, was driven from the city of Linn by the enemies of the family. Formally exiled, all his property—including his banks—confiscated by the Patronate, he merely retreated to Mars and there, from the banking institution which he had established as one of his several branches under foreign governments, he reached back to Linn through unsuspected subsidiaries and resumed business. As had many another astute person before him, he had foreseen the exile; and so the conspirators found little of the treasure they had expected to seize when they took over his buildings.

They had necessarily recoursed to taxes. These proved so burdensome at that particular time, that there was a great desire among business men for the return of Cosan Deglet. This desire—Tews noted in his studies—was cleverly stimulated from Mars by Cosan himself. At the proper moment, the representatives of the people formally invited Cosan back from exile, defeated an attempt on the part of the nobles to seize the government by force, and successfully installed Cosan as elected Lord Leader.

The lesson was not lost on the Patrons who were subsequently elected to the Lord Leadership. Cosan, even when he was officially only a Patron, was repeatedly consulted, and no action was ever taken which did not have his approval.

For thirty years, he was virtual lord of Linn. Tews recalled a visit he had paid to the old palace, where Cosan had lived. It was now a commercial building, but a brass plate at the entrance, bore an inscription:

Passerby
Once the house of Cosan Deglet. In
which not alone a great man, but
Knowledge herself had her home.

Pursuit of knowledge, and banking—these were the cornerstones of the Deglet power. So Lord Tews decided. At key moments, the family's banking interests provided such a compelling force that resistance was overcome. And, during all the years of their growth, their penchant for collecting art masterpieces and their association with learned men brought with it a personal regard and admiration, which sustained them through the dangerous repercussions of their occasional errors of judgment.

During the long months of study and aloneness that

79

followed his ostracism, Tews' mind dwelt many times on those two factors, and gradually he became critical of the life he had lived in Linn. He began to see the madness of it, and the endless skulduggery. He read with more and more amazement the letters of his mother, outlining what she was doing. It was a tale of endless cunnings, conspiracies and murders, written in a simple code that was effective because it was based on words the extra-original meanings of which were known only to his mother and himself.

His amazement became disgust, and disgust grew into the first comprehension of the greatness of the Deglet-Linn family, as compared to their opponents. "Something had to be done about that pack of ignorant thieves and power-hungry rascals!" Tews decided. "My stepfather, the Lord Leader, took firm action, which was right at the time."

He had a great insight. It was no longer the correct approach. The way to a unified universe was not through a continuation of absolute power for one man, or family. The old republic never had a chance, since the factions gave it none. But now, after decades of virtual non-party patriotism under the Lord Leader, it should be possible to restore the republic with the very good possibility that it would work. As a safeguard, members of the family must again become personally skilled in banking practice.

Tews decided: "I shall make it my personal interest to do all of these things if I can ever return to Linn."

The months dragged by.

In a routine fashion, Nellian advised Medron Linn that: "...in two weeks, your grandson, Lord Clane, will take up residence with his retinue in an apartment of the Joquin Temple, and will resume his studies to the end of becoming a scientist."

The old man was surprised when a special messenger arrived two days later in a small space boat—used for fast flights over the surface of the Earth. The carrier brought an invitation for the tutor to attend on the Lord Leader at the Capitoline Palace for a conference. "If possible," said the letter of invitation, "simply come with the messenger, and you will be returned to your home before nightfall."

Nellian wisely regarded the invitation as a command. Within two hours, he was ushered into the presence of Medron Linn. He noted the other's lined, tired face, was briefly startled; and then took a large chair near the window overlooking a garden vista.

The Lord Leader sat down facing the window, but the chair was only a momentary focal point for his movements. He was away from it more often than on it. He paced the floor, paused to face Clane's tutor, and then paced again. Presently, he would be sitting restlessly in his chair, only to be up again, pacing, pausing, and pacing once more.

In this wise, they discussed the future of Lord Clane Linn, sixteen years old.

"The biggest task we have," said Medron Linn, not for the first time, "will be to keep—uh—inimical forces from having him strangled."

Nellian remained discreetly silent on that remark. He had no illusions as to who the "inimical forces" were. The Lady Lydia, wife of Medron Linn, was the direct danger.

The Lord Leader paused again in his walking, and this time there was a thoughtful look on his face. "Ours has been a strange family," he said reminiscently. "We had the money lender, and then the shrewd Cosan Deglet, who single-handedly brought our line to its first Lord Leadership. We can pass lightly over Parilee the Elder—his weakness permitted the growth of strong opposing forces. But the crisis came in the great struggle for the control of the temples in the time of Parilee Deglet and of his brother Loran. These men were disliked because they were both apt to ride rough-shod over the foolish and the ignorant, and because each in his own way saw something which had gone almost un-noticed until that time—the growing power of the temples. The priest-politician, working through the highly suggestible temple congregations, more and more influenced the growing state, and almost always in a fashion that was unrealistic

81

and narrow-minded, designed solely to expand the supremacy of the temples. Both Parilee and Loran, as a deliberate policy—there is no doubt of this in my mind—waged wars which had as their secondary purpose keeping great bodies of men away from the temples and of simultaneously giving them a soldier's philosophy which cancelled out to some degree the temple rule. The groups that later aligned themselves with Raheinl enjoyed throughout their existence the support, open or secret, of the temple scientists, and it is a remarkable tribute to Loran, my father and his brother that they were able to maintain their power and prestige—even as they were hated—while this evergrowing temple force conspired against them. When you consider that, as youths, they were exiled for nearly fifteen years until they were both in their middle thirties, you can gain an understanding of the problems they faced. During that fifteen years, there was a Linnan law which placed the penalty of death upon anyone who so much as suggested that the Deglets be allowed to return to Linn. Several friends of our family were hanged, or beheaded, on this charge."

The Lord Leader stood grim for a moment, and he seemed to be feeling within himself the anguish of the death of men who had been executed so long ago. After a little, he shook himself as if to cast off the feeling, and he said:

"Parilee and Loran returned to Linn as part of the army leaders' revolt more than sixty years ago; and they were determined and unpleasant persons. They refused to place any confidence in the crowds that hysterically cheered their coming. In an atmosphere of murder and assassination, they held their power—once they attained it—by ruthless legal control. Parilee was the brilliant general, Loran the shrewd administrator, and it is natural that he should have brought upon himself the main anger of the enemies of the family. As Loran's son, I had many opportunities to observe his methods. They were rough but necessary, but it was not surprising that, despite all his precautions, he was assassinated. An uncle of the two men maintained the government until Parilee returned from Venus with several legions, and firmly re-established our family, with himself as Lord Leader. One of his first acts was to call me for a conference, and point out the trend of events. I was seventeen, and the only male Deglet heir in the direct line, and what he said alarmed me. He anticipated his own death before long, since he had many ailments, and that meant that I would be only a youngster still when the crisis came.

"And so, at seventeen, he made me co-Lord Leader with a view to establishing my legal right to power. I was twenty-two when he died, and within a few months the expected insurrection occured. Because of the unanticipated defection of part of the army, it proved even more dangerous than we had thought. And so it took eight years of civil war to break the deadlock."

The weary and aging ruler paused, then: "If possible, we must prevent such a disaster from transpiring when my time comes. And so, it is vital that we utilize the services of every member of the family. Even Clane must play a great role."

Nellian, who had been waiting patiently for the other's purpose to be revealed, said. "What do you have in mind for him?"

The Lord Leader hesitated; then he drew a deep breath, and said sharply: "We cannot wait until those old temple scientists complete his training. Since Joquin's death there has been a lack of enthusiasm for his presence, which reflects the old rebellion and the old intrigue. I should like you to ask Clane if he is prepared to assume immediately the mantle of Chief Scientist, and so become a member of the inner temple hierarchy?"

"At sixteen!" Nellian breathed. And that, for a while, was all he could think of saying.

Actually, he saw nothing wrong in the proposal that a sixteen-year-old should become one of the leaders of the temple. The pattern of family rights was as ingrained in him as it was in the Lord Leader. But, as an old temple follower, and supporter, he felt intensely unhappy at the purpose which was all too plainly apparent in the ruler, that of using Clane to subordinate the temples to the Linn family.

He thought uneasily: "If my training of the boy is effective, he will not be completely a family supporter, but will regard his role in the temples as having an importance and meaning all its own." Nevertheless, that was only a possibility. Clane had his own brand of arrogance.

Aloud, Nellian said finally: "Your excellency, intellectually, this boy is ready. Emotionally—" He shook his head.

The Lord Leader, who had been briefly seated, came up out of his chair, and walked forward until he stood directly in front of the tutor, looking down at him. He said in a deliberate tone: "By the atom gods, he must go through this experience also. And tell him from me that I will not tolerate his having only this girl Selk as his mistress. I cannot permit at this stage his remaining infatuated with any one woman. I don't mean he should discard her; simply, there must be others. And tell him that when he enters the Joquin temple ten days from now, he will enter as a Chief Scientist, and that I want him to act accordingly."

He turned away, in an attitude of finality; then swung about, and said: "I'll speak to you again about the dangers of assassination. Meanwhile, advise him to stay out of Lydia's way. That is all. You may depart."

He turned again, and this time he stalked out of the room.

After three months, Nellian received a second invitation to the Capitoline Palace; this time the Lord Leader seemed less tense.

"I've been hearing things about the boy," he said. "But I'd like direct information. What is this about the healing methods being used at his chief temple?"

The tutor frowned. "A most reprehensible practice," he said coldly. "However, Lord Clane has assured me that the purposes are purely experimental, so I am acting for him as a scientific observer."

The Lord Leader, who had been pacing the floor, paused and stared down at the old scholar, whose bushy brows were knit with disapproval. He was reminded that Nellian was a former republican, with certain republican views. Since the adherents of the republic had associated themselves with the pernicious temple practice of mass suggestion, their disapproval of anything at all was totally inadmissable to the Lord Leader. This was particularly true of matters having to do with the temples themselves.

He parted his lips to say so, thought better of it, and then said mildly: "What is it that is happening, and what is it that you disapprove of?"

Nellian said warmly: "Your grandson has long been interested in the temple rituals and their effect on so many people. So, as an experiment, he had transported to the Joquin temple, which he now heads—as you know—a very intricate-looking machine, rescued from an ancient digging. This machine had many dials on it and from the moment that it was installed it proved to be an object that evoked superstitious awe. To my amazement, your grandson announced to the congregation that it would heal the sick and the injured, but that they must first come and be registered on it. This meant, simply, that the ill person watched while a series of dials were set in his presence, ostensibly tuning him into its healing radiation. In my presence, I heard Lord Clane inform one individual that from that moment every sensation he felt in his body would derive from the machine, and that its healing power would be felt throughout each day and night."

The old scholar paused, quivering; then: "Your excellency, it hurt me to see your grandson so misuse the reverence of the people for the temples. Such cynicism is highly disturbing."

The Lord Leader brushed aside the criticism. "Well," he said, "what was the result? I do not trust the stories I heard, since they were too favorable. Did the—ah—machine heal the ill and the injured?"

"Of course, it did." Nellian was impatient. "But your excellency misses the point. The misuse of the worship in the temples for such worldly purpose is positively—" He groped for words—"sacrilegious."

Medron Linn studied the other curiously. "What you have told me tells me that Clane has enlarged the use of the suggestion rituals of the temples. In your opinion, how should those rituals be utilized?"

Nellian was firm. "For spiritual purposes. To lead the worldly men and women to greater reverence for the gods. Since people are suggestible, there must be a fundamental reason for it closely related to the god-given origin of life itself. To use it as a means of curing the flesh of its ailments—" He shuddered, and shook his head, and said with finality: "I will not be associated with such an experiment after the new year."

The Linn of Linn paced back and forth before the window, struggling to suppress a smile. He stopped finally, and asked soberly: "Does Clane perform all these rituals himself? It seems like a considerable task for one person."

The tutor shook his head, suddenly more cheerful. "He did at first, but as you know he long ago became a sort of protector of other mutations like himself. He has taken some of the more intelligent of these, and has taught them the rituals in connection with the machine. So it is they who now perform during the long hours, and your grandson actually visits the temple only once a week. What is worthwhile about this action is that people are beginning to feel a little differently about mutations. It will probably take quite a while for the change to become apparent to anyone above the lower classes, since Linn is full of cynics and scoffers. But there is a steady progression toward tolerance, still on a very small scale, of course. There must be some other way, however, to win goodwill for mutations."

"What would you suggest?" asked the Lord Leader, gently.

"I have nothing in mind at the moment," said Nellian testily, "but I have no doubt that a method could be devised which would not include such a base misuse of suggestion."

The other man nodded thoughtfully, and said finally in a serious tone: "I have great respect for you, Nellian, as you know. But I am greatly troubled by this mutation problem. I should like very much if you would tolerate this activity of my grandson, and that in the meanwhile you would give thought to some other method for achieving the same ends—that is, acceptance of mutations by the great mass of people....Let us not worry about the attitude of the upper classes." He finished smoothly: "As soon as you have developed an alternative method, come to me, and—if it seems practicable—you shall have my support in presenting it to the people."

Nellian nodded grimly. "Very well, your excellency. I do not wish to seem too inflexible, and I am actually noted for my general tolerance—but this is too much for a man of principle. I will devise such a method as you have requested, and will present it to you in due course. You have my best wishes, sir."

Medron Linn called after him: "Tell Clane to stay out of sight when my wife is around."

The tutor paused on his way to the door, and turned gravely. "Very well, your excellency."

The Lord Leader said wryly: "As for this machine that heals one on a twenty-four hour a day basis—my only regret is that I am not myself suggestible. I could use a little simpleness of mind at this period of my life."

Nellian said: "Why not come to the temples in a more orthodox fashion, sir? I'm sure the gods could give comfort even to the noblest minds."

"There we are in disagreement," was the sardonic reply. "It is a well-known fact that the atom gods are interested only in the ignorant, the simple, the believing—and of course in their faithful servants, the temple scientists. Good day, sir."

He turned and walked stiffly out of the room.

11

One day, as Clane was walking along a street of Linn with the Martian slave girl, Selk, as his companion—a guard followed discreetly fifty feet behind—he came upon a young artist painting. Clane stopped.

The man had a quick, friendly smile for his watchers, and then he continued with deft strokes to work on his canvas. The painting was a joyous swirl of colors, somehow contriving to bring out an amazing representation of the street and its buildings. Clane, whose artistic education was largely religious, was astonished. "How much?" he asked.

"Five hundred sesterces."

The mutation paid half of the amount, and said: "When the painting is completed, bring it to my house." He wrote his name and address on a card, and handed it to the young man, who raised his eyebrows when he saw what was written there but said nothing.

He arrived at Clane's town house the following afternoon, accompanied by a dark-haired, intense girl and a stocky, uncombed young man. They were all three affable young people, delighted with the painting, and prepared to discuss in detail the exact nature of the frame it should be put in. On impulse, and feeling completely at ease, Clane invited them to remain for dinner.

During the wait for the meal to be prepared and served, he was particularly aware of the girl. She moved restlessly about, carrying the mixed drink which she had chosen at the bar, and had mixed herself. She refused to be served by a slave.

"I don't believe in slavery," she announced coolly in front of three slaves. "I think it's an abominable and barbarous practice."

Clane said nothing to that. He was familiar with the arguments against slavery, but he knew how dangerous a subject it was politically. So he continued to watch his female guest, and presently noticed that she was actually examining all the costly drapes and the fine furniture. She had just picked up one end of a priceless carpet, and felt it with her fingers, when she grew aware of his gaze upon her. She came over and said:

"I'll have to bring the matter up, or it will be a barrier between us. You're the mutation Linn?"

He felt a chill...instantaneous. But there was too much affinity in her manner for the paralysis to hold. He inclined his head, and for the first time in his life he described his affliction out loud: "The atom gods marked me with a poor rib-cage, twisted arms and skimpy shoulders."

"Does it bother you?" she asked. "It doesn't me."

Before Clane could make any comment, dinner was announced. Since it would be entirely served by slaves, he watched to see her reactions. But if she realized the paradox, she showed no sign. Evidently, having made her point, she was not prepared to force an impossible issue.

During the meal, it developed that the uncombed one was a composer. "If you wish," he said, "I'll compose a dinner piece in honor of this occasion, and dedicate it to you."

Clane was interested. "What instruments would predominate in such a composition?" he asked.

"Strings."

"Compose it!" said Clane. "I'll be very happy to pay you for it, and have a string orchestra come here and play it for us."

"Pay for it!" said the young man. He sounded outraged.

The girl said quickly: "Oh, we can get together an orchestra, but I think it would be delightful if you did pay Medda. He's such a fool about money. His folks are merchants, and ever since his father disowned him for becoming a musician, he's been pretending money is unimportant."

Medda scowled at her, then turned to Clane. "Your excellency," he said, "this girl has a beautiful voice and a splendid figure, and she is an excellent plucker of various stringed instruments. But she has never learned to mind her own business."

The girl ignored him. She addressed Clane: "How much would you pay him for a ten minute dinner piece that really had power, excitement and melody?"

Clane smiled. "How about five hundred sesterces?"

The girl clapped her hands. "It's a bargain," she said. "Medda, you'll eat for a month."

Medda muttered something, but he did not really look displeased. He agreed presently to deliver the finished composition in one week.

Later, as they were leaving, the girl lingered in the outer hallway, and said to Clane: "I've heard you live a very studious life, surrounded by old men and slaves. Why not meet more of the younger artists, and find out what people are creating today, not only what they created a hundred years ago?"

The realization had already dawned on Clane. He did not make the error at that moment of dismissing the past, but the evening had been a pleasant surprise to him. Before he could reply, the girl spoke again, in a lowered tone.

"There're some wonderfully talented young men among the artists around the city, and some very talented and attractive girls, including me." She smiled, and stepped back for him to look at her.

She was such a new type of personality, and so fresh looking physically, that Clane was shaken by her attitude. He said at last, with an effort: "Delightfully attractive."

She smiled with pleasure, and said: "I'm sure that the girls would be willing to include you as one of the group. But we have a rule, your excellency, which we do not break for anyone. During the period that you associate with us, there must be no slave girls. Goodbye."

She turned, and walked lightly out of the door to where her companions waited. The three of them moved off along the torch-lighted walk.

Alone, Clane evaluated his visitors. He guessed that he had contacted representatives of an impecunious artists' colony, and guessed also that a man who gave even an occasional five hundred sesterces would be a welcome addition to their ranks.

Could he afford to involve himself? Theoretically, as a Chief Scientist, he should be a person who lived an ascetic existence.

As the Linn mutation, whose main task was to gain ascendancy over his own compulsive behaviour, it might be well worth his while to become—he smiled at certain incongruities of the notion—a patron of the arts.

The growing youth stayed out of Lydia's way as a matter of policy, carefully and consciously. When she was at her home in the city of Linn, Clane spent months at his country estate rather than risk being seen by the Lord Leader's wife. Only when she retired to one of the remoter palaces did he take up residence in his town house.

By maintaining his distance, he could candidly estimate her danger to him. At no time during those years before he attained his majority did he have any real fear of Lady Lydia. He simply knew her for what she was, and acted accordingly.

It was a period of learning for him. He exhausted the resources of education at the temples and in Joquin's library. The great scholars who came by invitation to his home were one by one stripped of their ideas and their knowledge, at least of as much of it as they would impart. Among the many interesting things he learned was the fact that one of the greatest repositories of knowledge in the realm was his grandfather's library at the Capitoline Palace.

There—he was told—he would be able to find many unobtainable books of olden days, collected for a hundred years by agents for the Deglets and Linns from all over the solar system. According to his informant, some of the books had never been read during the lifetime of any man now living. This was due to the fact that the Lord Leader had reserved them for his old age in the belief that he would then have the time to catch up on his learning. As was to be expected of so busy an individual, the time never arrived.

Clane waited until Lady Lydia left the city for one of her periodic rests. Then he established residence in Linn, and requested of the Lord Leader permission to read the rare books. The great man, whose interest in such projects had long declined almost to vanishment, granted the permission —and so Clane, and three secretary-slaves (two men and a woman) for some weeks, daily entered the palace library and read about the superstitions of a transitional period of history. The books had, in every case, been written *after* the legendary golden age, but before all details about such a period of human development were generally dismissed as nonsensical lies.

The books added very little data to what he already know, but their authors reported the hearsay that had come by father through son for many generations from mistier days. The stories pointed a direction. They added to his certainty that he was on a trail that might lead to even more valuable discoveries than he had already made.

He was intently engaged one day in the pursuit of reading still another book when, on looking up to rest his eyes, he saw his step-grandmother come into the library. It was his first knowledge that she was back in the city.

For the Lady Lydia, the meeting was as unexpected as it was for Clane. She had almost forgotten that he existed, having returned to Linn because of a report from her husband's physician that the Lord Leader was ailing. It was the kind of report that brought home to her the realization that she must waste no more time in her purpose of persuading the old man that Tews should be brought back from exile.

She saw Clane now for the first time under conditions that were favorable to his appearance. He was modestly attired in the fatigue gown of a temple scientist, a costume that was effective for covering up his physical deformities.

There were folds of cloth to conceal his mutated arms so skillfully that his normal human hands came out into the open as if they were the natural extensions of a healthy boy. The cloak was drawn up into a narrow, not unattractive band around his neck, which served to hide the subtly mutated shoulders and the unhuman chest formation. Above the collar, Lord Clane's head reared with all the pride of a young lordling.

It was a head to make any woman look twice, delicately beautiful, with a remarkably clear skin. Lydia, who had never seen her husband's grandson, except at a distance— Clane had made sure of that—felt a constricting fear in her heart.

"By Uranium!" she thought. "Another great man. As if I didn't have enough trouble trying to get Tews back from exile."

It hardly seemed likely that death would be necessary for a mutation. But if she ever hoped to have Tews inherit the empire, then all the more direct heirs would have to be taken care of in some way. Standing there, she added this new relative to her list of the more dangerous kin of the ailing Lord Leader.

She saw that Clane was looking at her. His face had changed, stiffened, lost some of its good looks, and that brought a memory of things she had heard about him. That he was easily upset emotionally. The prospect interested her. She walked towards him, a thin smile on her long, handsome countenance.

Twice, as she stood tall before him, he tried to get up. And failed each time. All the color was gone from his cheeks, his face even more strained looking than it had been, ashen and unnatural, twisted, changed, the last shape of vistage beauty gone from it. His lips worked with the effort of speech, but only a muted burst of unintelligible sounds issued forth.

Lydia grew aware that the young slave woman secretary

was almost as agitated as her master. The creature looked beseechingly at Lydia, finally gasped, "May I speak, your excellency?"

That shocked her. Slaves didn't speak except when spoken to. It was not just a rule or regulation dependent upon the whim of the particular owner: it was the law of the land, and anybody could report a breach as a misdemeanor, and collect half the fine which was subsequently levied from the slave's master. What dazed Lady Lydia was that *she* should have been the victim of such a degrading experience. She was so stunned that the young woman had time to gasp: "You must forgive him. He is subject to fits of nervous paralysis, when he can neither move nor speak. The sight of his illustrious grandmother coming upon him by surprise—"

That was as far as she got. Lydia found her voice. She snapped, "It's too bad that all slaves are not similarly afflicted. How dare you speak to me?"

She stopped, catching herself sharply. It was not often that she lost her temper, and she had no intention of letting the situation get out of hand. The slave girl was sagging away as if she had been struck with a violence beyond her power to resist. Lydia watched the process of disintegration curiously. There was only one possible explanation for the slave speaking up so boldly for her master. She must be one of his favorite mistresses. And the odd thing, in this case, was that the slave herself seemed to approve of the relationship, or she wouldn't have been so anxious for him.

It would appear, thought Lydia, *that this mutation relative of mine can make himself attractive in spite of his deformities, and that it isn't only a case of a slave girl compelled by her circumstances.*

It seemed to her that the moment had potentialities. "What," she said, "is your name?"

"Selk," The young woman spoke huskily.

"Oh, a Martian."

The Martian war, some years before, had produced some

94

hundreds of thousands of husky, goodlooking boy and girl Martians for the slave schools to train.

Lydia's plan grew clear. She would have the girl assassinated, and so put the first desperate fear into the mutation. That should hold him until she had succeeded in bringing Tews back from exile to supreme power. After all, he was not too important. It would be impossible for a despised mutation to ever become Lord Leader. He had to be put out of the way in the long run, because the Linn party would otherwise try to make use of him against Tews and herself.

She paused for a last look down at Clane. He was sitting rigid, his eyes glazed, his face still colorless and unnatural. She made no effort to conceal her contempt as, with a flounce of her skirt, she turned and walked away, followed by her ladies and personal slaves.

Slaves were sometimes trained to be assassins. The advantage of using them was that they could not be witnesses in court either for or against the accused. But Lydia had long discovered that, if anything went wrong, if a crisis arose as a result of the murder attempt, a slave assassin did not have the same determination to win over obstacles. Slaves took to their heels at the slightest provocation, and returned with fantastic accounts of the odds that had defeated them. She used former knights and sons of knights, whose families had been degraded from their rank because they were penniless. Such men had a desperate will to acquire money, and when they failed she could usually count on learning the reason.

She had a horror of not knowing the facts. For more than thirty of her sixty years her mind had been an unsaturable sponge for details and ever more details. It was accordingly of more than ordinary interest to her when the two knights she had hired to murder her stepgrandson's slave girl, Selk, reported that they had been unable to find the girl.

"There is no such person now attached to Lord Clane's city household."

Her informant, a slim youth named Meerl, spoke with

that mixture of boldness and respect which the more devil-may-care assassins affected when talking to high personages. "Lady," he went on with a bow and a smile, "I think you have been outwitted."

"I'll do the thinking," said Lydia with asperity. "You're a sword or a knife with a strong arm to wield it. Nothing more."

"And a good brain to direct it," said Meerl.

Lydia scarcely heard. Her retort had been almost automatic. Because—could it be? Was it possible that Clane had realized what she would do?

What startled her was the decisiveness of it, the prompt action that had been taken on the basis of what would only have been a suspicion. The world was full of people who never did anything about their suspicions. If Clane had consciously frustrated her, then he was even more dangerous than she had thought. She'd have to plan her next move with care.

She grew aware that the two men were still standing before her. She glared at them. "Well, what are you waiting for? You know there is no money if you fail."

"Gracious lady," said Meerl, "we did not fail. You failed."

Lydia hesitated, impressed by the fairness of the thrust. She had a certain grudging respect for this particular assassin. "Fifty per cent," she said.

She tossed forward a pouch of money. It was skillfully caught. The men bowed quickly, stiffly, with a flash of white teeth and clank of steel. They whirled and disappeared through thick portieres that concealed the door by which they had entered.

Lydia sat alone with her thoughts, but not for long. A knock came on another door, and one of her ladies-in-waiting entered, holding a sealed letter in her hand.

"This arrived, madam, while you were engaged."

Lydia's eyebrows went up a little when she saw that the letter was from Clane. She read it, tight-lipped:

To my most gracious grandmother
Honorable lady:

I offer my sincere apologies for the insult and distress which I caused your ladyship yesterday in the library. I can only plead that my nervous afflictions are well-known in the family, and that, when I am assailed, it is beyond my power to control myself.

I also offer apologies for the action of my slave girl in speaking to you. It was my first intention to turn her over to you for punishment. But then it struck me that you were so tremendously busy at all times, and besides she scarcely merited your attention. Accordingly, I have had her sold in the country to a dealer in labor, and she will no doubt learn to regret her insolence.

With renewed humble apologies, I remain,

Your obedient grandson,

Clane

Reluctantly, the Lady Linn was compelled to admire the letter. Now she would never know whether she had been outwitted or victorious.

I suppose, she thought acridly, *I could at great expense discover if he merely sent her to his country estate, there to wait until I have forgotten what she looks like. Or could I even do that?*

She paused to consider the difficulties. She would have to send as an investigator someone who had seen the girl. Who? She looked up. "Dalat."

The woman who had brought the letter curtsied.

"Yes?"

"What did that slave girl in the library yesterday look like?"

Dalat was disconcerted. "W-why, I don't think I noticed, your ladyship. A blonde, I think."

"A blonde!" Explosively. "Why, you numbskull. That girl had the most fancy head of golden hair that I've seen in many years—and you didn't notice!"

97

Dalat was herself again. "I am not accustomed to remembering slaves," she said.

"Get out of here," said Lydia. But she said it in a flat tone, without emotion. Here was defeat.

She shrugged finally. After all, it was only an idea she had had. Her problem was to get Tews back to Linn. Lord Clane, the only mutation ever born into the family of the Lord Leader, could wait.

Nevertheless, the failure rankled.

12

The Lord Leader had over a period of years become an ailing old man, who could not make up his mind. At seventy-one, he was almost blind in his left eye, and only his voice remained strong. He had a thunderous baritone that still struck terror into the hearts of criminals when he sat on the chair of high judgment, a duty which, because of its sedentary nature, he cultivated more and more as the swift months of his declining years passed by.

The work had another characteristic. On occasion, after he had made up his mind on a matter—although the counsel for the opposing sides were still wrangling—he allowed his thoughts to wander to the ever more pressing problem of the future of the family.

"The fact is," he decided one afternoon, "I must see all those young people personally, and estimate their value as Lord Leader material."

Quite consciously, he included the mutation among those whom he planned to visit.

That night he made the mistake of sitting on the balcony

too long without a blanket. He caught a cold, and spent the whole of the month that followed in bed. It was there, helpless on his back, acutely aware of his weak body, fully, clearly aware at last that he had at most a few years to live, that the Lord Leader realized finally that he could delay no longer in selecting an heir. In spite of his personal dislike for Tews, he found himself listening, at first grudgingly, then more amenably, to his wife.

"Remember," she said, again and again, "your dream of bequeathing to the world a unified empire. Surely, you cannot become sentimental about it at the last minute. Lords Jerrin and Draid are still too young. Jerrin, of course, is the most brilliant young man of his generation. He is obviously a future Lord Leader, and should be named so in your will. But not yet. You cannot hand over the solar system to a youngster of twenty-four."

The Lord Leader stirred uneasily. He noticed that there was not a word in her argument about the reason for Tews' exile. And that she was too clever ever to allow into her voice the faintest suggestion that, behind her logic, was the emotional fact that Tews was her son.

"There are of course," Lydia continued, "the boy's uncles on their mother's side, both amiable administrators but lacking in will."

She paused. "And then there are your daughters and sons-in-law, and their children."

"Forget them." The Lord Leader, gaunt and intent on the pillow, moved a hand weakly in dismissal of the suggestion. He was not interested in the second-raters. "You have forgotten," he said finally, "Clane."

"A mutation!" said Lydia, surprised. "Are you serious?"

The Lord of Linn was silent. He knew better, reluctantly. But he knew why he had made the suggestion. Delay. He realized he was being pushed inexorably to choosing as his heir Lydia's plumpish son by her first husband.

"If you considered your own blood only," urged Lydia, "it would be just another case of imperial succession so common among our tributary monarchies and among the barbarians of Aiszh and Venus and Mars. Politically it would be meaningless. If, however, you strike across party lines, your action will speak for your supreme patriotism. In no other way could you so finally and unanswerably convince the world that you have only its interest at heart."

The old scoundrel, dimmed though his spirit and intellect were by illness and age, was not quite so simple as that. He knew what they were saying under the pillars, that Lydia was molding him like a piece of putty to her plans. Not that such opinions disturbed him very much. The tireless propaganda of his enemies and of mischief makers and gossips had dinned into his ears for nearly fifty years, and he had become immune to the chatter.

In the end the decisive factor was only partly Lydia's arguments, and partly his own desperate realization that he had little choice. The unexpected factor was a visit to his bedside by the younger of his two daughters by his first marriage. She asked that he grant her a divorce from her present husband, and permit her to marry the exiled Tews.

"I have always," she said, "been in love with Tews, and only Tews, and I am willing to join him in exile."

The prospect was so dazzling that, for once, the old man was completely fooled. It did not even occur to him that Lydia had spent two days convincing the cautious Gudrun that here was her only chance of becoming first lady of Linn.

"Otherwise," Lydia had pointed out, "you'll be just another relative, dependent upon the whim of the reigning Lord Leader's wife."

The Linn of Linn suspected absolutely nothing of that behind-the-scenes connivance. His daughter married to Lord Tews! The possibilities warmed his chilling blood. She was too old, of course, to have any more children, but she would serve Tews as Lydia had him, a perfect foil, a perfect representative of his own political group. *His* daughter!

I must, he thought, *go and see what Clane thinks. Meanwhile I can send for Tews on a tentative basis.*

He didn't say that out loud. No one in the family except himself realized the enormous extent of the knowledge that the long-dead temple scientist Joquin had bequeathed to Clane. The Lord Leader preferred to keep the information in his own mind. He knew Lydia's propensity for hiring assassins, and it wouldn't do to subject Clane to more than ordinary danger from that source.

He regarded the mutation as an unsuspected stabilizing force during the chaos that might follow his death. He wrote a letter inviting Tews to return to Linn, and, a week later, finally out of bed, he had himself carried to Clane's residence in the west suburbs. He remained overnight, and, returning the next day, began to discharge a score of key men whom Lydia had slipped into administrative positions on occasions when he was too weary to know what the urgent business was for which he was signing papers.

Lydia said nothing, but she noted the sequence of events. A visit to Clane, then action against her men. She pondered that for some days, and then, the day before Tews was due, she set out on her first visit to the modest looking home of Lord Clane Linn, taking care that she was not expected.

On the way, it occurred to her that she was not satisfied with her situation. A dozen of her schemes were coming to a head; and here she was going to see Lord Clane, a completely unknown factor. Thinking about it from that viewpoint, she felt astonished. What possible danger, she asked herself again and again, could a mutation be to her?

Even as those thoughts infuriated the surface of her mind, deep inside, she knew better. There was something here. The old man would never bother with a nonentity. He was either quiet with the quietness of weariness, or utterly impatient. Young people particularly enraged him easily, and if Clane were an exception, then there was a reason.

From a distance, Clane's residence looked small. There was brush in the foreground, and a solid wall of trees across the entire eight-hundred foot front of the estate. The house peaked a few feet above a mantle of pines and evergreens. As her chair drew nearer, Lydia decided it was a three-story building, which was certainly minuscule beside the palaces of the other Linns. Her bearers puffed up a hill, trotted past a

101

pleasant arbor of trees, and came after a little to a low, massive fence that had not been visible from below. Lydia, always alert for military obstacles, had her chair put down.

She climbed out, conscious that a cool, sweet breeze was blowing where, a moment before, had been only the dead heat of a stifling summer day. The air was rich with the perfume of trees and green things.

She walked slowly along the fence, noting that it was skillfully hidden from the street below by an unbroken hedge, although it showed through at this close range. She recognized the material as similar to that of which the temples of the scientists was constructed, only there was no visible lead lining. She estimated the height of the fence at three feet, and its thickness about three and half. It was fat and squat and defensively useless.

When I was young, she thought, *I could have jumped over it myself.* She returned to the chair, annoyed because she couldn't fathom its purpose, and yet couldn't quite believe it had no purpose. It was even more disconcerting to discover a hundred feet farther along the walk that the gate was not a closure but an opening in the wall, and that there was no guard in sight. In a minute more, the bearers had carried her inside, through a tunnel of interwoven shrubs shadowed by towering trees, and then to an open lawn. That was where the real surprise began.

"Stop!" said the Lady Lydia.

An enormous combination meadow and garden spread from the edge of the trees. She had an eye for size, and, without thinking about it, she guessed that fifteen acres were visible from her vantage point. A gracious stream meandered diagonally across the meadow. Along its banks scores of guest homes had been built, low, sleek, be-windowed structures, each with its overhanging shade trees. The house, a square-built affair, towered to her right. At the far end of the grounds were five spaceships neatly laid out side by side. And everywhere were people. Men and women singly and in groups, sitting in chairs, walking, working, reading, writing, drawing and painting. Thoughtfully, Lydia walked over to a painter, who sat with his easel and palette a scant dozen yards from her. She was not accustomed to being ignored.

She said sharply, "What is all this?" She waved an arm to take in the activities of the estate. "What is going on here?"

The young man shrugged. He dabbed thoughtfully at the scene he was painting, then, still without looking up said, "Here, madam, you have the center of Linn. Here the thought and opinion of the empire is created and cast into molds for public consumption. Ideas born here, once they are spread among the masses, become the mores of the nation and the solar system. To be invited here is an unequaled honor, for it means that your work as a scholar or artist has received the ultimate recognition that power and money can give. Madam, whoever you are, I welcome you to the intellectual center of the world. You would not be here if you had not some unsurpassed achievement to your credit. However, I beg of you, please do not tell what it is until this evening when I shall be happy to lend you both my ears. And now, old and successful woman, good day to you."

Lydia withdrew thoughtfully. Her impulse, to have the young man stripped and lashed, yielded before a sudden desire to remain incognito as long as possible while she explored this unsuspected outdoor salon.

It was a universe of strangers. Not once did she see a face she recognized. These people, whatever their achievements, were not the publicized great men of the empire. She saw no patrons and only one man with the insignia of a knight on his coat. And when she approached him, she recognized from the alien religious symbol connected with the other markings, that his knighthood was of provincial origin. He was standing near a fountain which spewed forth a skillfully blended mixture of water and smoke. It made a pretty show, the smoke rising up in a thin streamlike cloud. As she paused beside the fountain there was a cessation of the cooling breeze, and she felt a wave of heat that reminded her of the steaming hot lower town. Lydia concentrated on the man and on her desire for information.

"I'm new here," she said engagingly. "Has this center been long in operation?"

"About five years, madam. After all, our young prince is only twenty-four!"

"Prince?" asked Lydia.

The knight, a rugged-faced individual, was apologetic.

"I beg your pardon. It is an old word of my province, signifying a leader of high birth. I discovered on my various journeys into the pits, where the atom gods live, and where once cities existed, that the name was of legendary origin. This is according to old books I found in remnants of buildings."

Lydia said, shocked: "You went down into one of the reputed homes of the gods, where the eternal fires burn?"

The knight chuckled. "Some of them are less eternal than others, I discovered."

"But weren't you afraid of being physically damaged?"

"Madam," shrugged the other, "I am over fifty years old. Why should I worry if my blood is slightly damaged by the aura of the gods."

Lydia hesitated, interested. But she had let herself be drawn from her purpose. "Prince," she repeated now, grimly. Applied to Clane, the title had a ring she didn't like. Prince Clane. It was rather stunning to discover that there were men who thought of him as a leader. What had happened to the old prejudices against mutations? She was about to speak again when, for the first time, she actually looked at the fountain.

She pulled back with a gasp. The water was bubbling. A mist of steam arose from it. Her gaze shot up to the spout, and now she saw that it was not smoke and water spewing up from it. It was boiling, steaming water. Water that roiled and rushed and roared. More hot water than she had ever seen from an artificial source. Memory came of the blackened pots in which slaves heated her daily hot water needs. And she felt a spurt of pure jealousy at the extravagant luxury of a fountain of boiling water on one's grounds.

"But how does he do it?" she gasped. "Has he tapped an underground hot spring?"

"No, madam, the water comes from the stream over there." The knight pointed. "It is brought here in tiled pipes, and then runs off into the various guest homes."

"Is there some arrangement of hot coals?"

"Nothing, madam." The knight was beginning to enjoy himself visibly. "There is an opening under the fountain, and you can look in if you wish."

Lydia wished. She was fascinated. She realized she had let herself be distracted, but for the moment that was of secondary importance. She watched with bright eyes as the knight opened the little door in the cement, and then she stooped beside him to peer in. It took several seconds to become accustomed to the dim light inside, but finally she was able to make out the massive base of the spout, and the six-inch pipe that ran into it. Lydia straightened slowly. The man shut the door matter-of-factly. As he turned, she asked, "But how does it work?"

The knight shrugged. "Some say that the water gods of Mars have been friendly to him ever since they helped his late father to win the war against the Martians. You will recall that the canal waters boiled in a frightful fury, thus confusing the Martians as they were attacked. And then again, others say that it is the atom gods helping their favorite mutation."

"Oh!" said Lydia. This was the kind of talk she could understand. She had never in her life worried about what the gods might think of her actions. And she was not going to start now. She straightened and glared imperiously at the man.

"Don't be such a fool," she said. "A man who has dared to penetrate the homes of the gods should have more sense than to repeat old wives' tales like that."

The man gaped. She turned away before he could speak, and marched off to her chair. "To the house!" she commanded her slaves. They had her at the front entrance of the residence before it struck her that she had not learned the tremendous and precious secret of the boiling fountains.

She caught Clane by surprise. She entered the house in her flamboyant manner, and by the time a slave saw her, and ran to his master's laboratory to bring the news of her coming, it was too late. She loomed in the doorway, as Clane turned from a corpse he was dissecting. To her immense disappointment he did not freeze up in one of his emotional spasms. She had expected it, and her plan was to look over the laboratory quietly and without interference.

But Clane came towards her. "Honorable grandmother," he said. And knelt to kiss her hand. He came up with an easy grace. "I hope," he said with an apparent eagerness, "that you will have the time and inclination to see my home and my work. Both have interesting features."

His whole manner was so human, so engaging, that she was disconcerted anew, not an easy emotion for her to experience. She shook off the weakness impatiently. Her first words affirmed her purpose in visiting him. "Yes," she said, "I shall be happy to see your home. I have been intending for some years to visit you, but I have been so busy." She sighed. "The duties of statecraft can be very onerous."

The beautiful face looked properly sympathetic. A delicate hand pointed at the dead body, which those slim fingers had been working over. The soft voice informed that the purpose of the dissection was to discover the position pattern of the organs and muscles and bones.

"I have cut open dead mutations," Clane said, "and compared them with normal bodies."

Lydia could not quite follow the purpose. After all, each mutation was different, depending upon the way the god forces had affected them. She said as much. The glowing blue eyes of the mutation looked at her speculatively.

"It is commonly known," he said, "that mutations seldom live beyond the age of thirty. Naturally," he continued with a faint smile, "since I am within six years of that milestone, the possibility weighs upon me. Joquin, that astute old scientist, who unfortunately is now dead, believed that the deaths resulted from inner tensions, due to the manner in which mutations were treated by their fellows. He felt that if those tensions could be removed, as they have been to some extent in me, a normal span of life would follow as also would normal intelligence. I'd better correct that. He believed that a mutation, given a chance, would be able to realize his normal *potentialities,* which might be either super- or sub-normal compared to human beings."

Clane smiled. "So far," he said, "I have noticed nothing out of the ordinary in myself."

Lydia thought of the boiling fountain, and felt a chill. *That old fool, Joquin,* she thought in a cold fury. *Why didn't I pay more attention to what he was doing? He's created an alien mind in our midst within striking distance of the top of the power group of the empire.*

The sense of immense disaster possibilities grew. *Death,* she thought, *within hours after the old man is gone. No risks can be taken with this creature.*

Suddenly, she was interested in nothing but the accessibility of the various rooms of the house to assassins. Clane seemed to realize her mood, for after a brief tour of the laboratory, of which she remembered little, he began the journey from room to room. Now, her eyes and attention sharpened. She peered into doors, examined windows, and did not fail to note with satisfaction the universal carpeting of the floors. Meerl would be able to attack without warning sounds.

"And your bedroom?" she asked finally.

"We're coming to it," said Clane. "It's downstairs, adjoining the laboratory. There's something else in the lab that I want to show you. I wasn't sure at first that I would, but now"—his smile was angelic—"I will."

The corridor that led from the living room to the bedroom was almost wide enough to be an ante-room. The walls were hung with drapes from floor to ceiling, which was odd. Lydia, who had no inhibitions, lifted one drape, and peered under it. The wall was vaguely warm, like an ember, and it was built of temple stone. She looked at Clane questioningly.

"I have some god metals in the house. Naturally, I am taking no chances. There's another corridor leading from the laboratory to the bedroom."

What interested Lydia was that neither door of the bedroom had either a lock or a bolt on it. She thought about that tensely, as she followed Clane through the ante-room that led to the laboratory. He wouldn't, it seemed to her, leave himself so unprotected forever. The assassins must strike before he grew alarmed, the sooner the better. Regretfully, she decided it would have to be after Tews was confirmed as heir to the throne. She grew aware that Clane had paused beside a dark box.

"Gelo Greeant," he said, "brought this to me from one of his journeys into the realms of the gods. I'm going to step inside, and you go around to the right there, and look into the dark glass. You will be amazed."

Lydia obeyed, puzzled. For a moment, after Clane had disappeared inside, the glass remained dark. Then it began to glow faintly. She retreated a step before that alien shiningness, then, remembering who she was, stood her ground.

And then she screamed.

A skeleton glowed through the glass. And the shadow of a beating heart, the shadow of expanding and contracting lungs. As she watched, petrified now, the skeleton arm moved, and seemed to come towards her, but drew back again. At last comprehension came to her paralyzed brain.

She was looking at the inside of a living human being. At Clane. Abruptly, that interested her. *Clane.* Like lightning, her eyes examined the bone structure. She noticed the cluster of ribs around his heart and lungs, the special thickness of his collar bones. Her gaze flashed down towards his kidneys, but this time she was too slow. The light faded, and went out. Clane emerged from the box.

"Well," he asked, pleased, "what do you think of my little gift from the gods?"

The phraseology startled Lydia. All the way home she thought of it. Gift from the gods! In a sense it was. The atom gods had sent their mutation a method of seeing himself, for studying his own body. What could *their* purpose be? She had a conviction that, if the gods really existed, and if, as seemed evident, they were helping Clane, then the Deities of the Atom were again—as they had in legendary times—interfering with human affairs.

The sinking sensation that came had only one hopeful rhythm. And that was like a drumbeat inside her: Kill! And soon. *Soon.*

But the days passed. And the demands of political stability absorbed all her attention. Nevertheless, in the midst of a score of new troubles, she did not forget Clane.

The messenger from the Lord Leader inviting Tews' return arrived on the same ship as another letter from his mother. Hers sounded as if it had been written in breathless haste, but it contained an explanation of how his recall had been accomplished. The price shocked Tews.

What, he thought, *marry Gudrun!*

It took an hour for his nerves to calm sufficiently for him even to consider the proposition. His plan, it seemed to him finally, was too important to be allowed to fail because of his distaste for a woman whose interest in men ran not so much to quality as to quantity. And it wasn't as if he were bound to another woman. His wife, seven years before, on discovering that his departure from Linn might be permanent, hastily persuaded her father to declare them divorced. Yes, he was free to marry.

The return of Tews was a triumph for his mother's diplomacy and a great moment for himself. His ship came down in the square of the pillars, and there, before an immense cheering throng, he was welcomed by the Lord Leader and the entire patronate. The parade that followed was led by a unit of five thousand glitteringly arrayed horse-mounted troops, followed by ten thousand foot soldiers, one thousand engineers and scores of mechanical engines for throwing weights and rocks at defensive barriers. Then came the Lord Leader, Lydia and Tews, and the three hundred patrons and six hundred knights of the empire. The rear of the parade was brought up by another cavalry unit of five thousand men.

From the rostrum that jutted out from the patronate building, the Lord Leader, his lion's voice undimmed by age, welcomed his stepson. All the lies that had ever been told about the reason for Tews' exile were coolly and grandly confirmed now. He had gone away to meditate. He had wearied of the cunnings and artifices of government. He had returned only after repeated pleadings on the part of his mother and of the Lord Leader.

"As you know," concluded the Lord Leader, "seven years ago, I was bereft of my natural heir in the moment of greatest military triumph the empire has ever experienced, the conquest of the Martians. Today, as I stand before you, no longer young, no longer able to bear the full weight of either military or political command, it is an immeasurable relief to me to be able to tell the people with confidence and conviction: Here in this modest and unassuming member of my family, the son of my dear wife, Lydia, I ask you to put your trust. To the soldiers I say, this is no weakling. Remember the Cimbri, conquered under his skillful generalship when he was but a youth of twenty-five. Particularly, I direct my words to the hard-pressed soldiers on Venus, where false leaders have misled the island provinces of the fierce Venusian tribes to an ill-fated rebellion. Ill-fated, I say, because as soon as possible Tews will be there with the largest army assembled by the empire since the war of the Martians. I am going to venture a prediction. I am going to predict that within two years the Venusian leaders will be hanging on long lines of posts of the type they are now using to murder prisoners. I predict that these hangings will be achieved by *Co-Lord Leader* General Tews, whom I now publicly appoint my heir and successor, and on whose behalf I now say, take warning, all those who would have ill befall the empire. Here is the man who will confound you and your schemes."

The dazzled Tews, who had been advised by his mother to the extent of the victory she had won for him, stepped forward to acknowledge the cheers and to say a few words. "Not too much," his mother had warned him. "Be non-

110

committal." But Lord Tews had other plans. He had carefully thought out the pattern of his future actions, and he had one announcement to make, in addition to a ringing acceptance of the military leadership that had been offered him, and a promise that the Venusian leaders would indeed suffer the fate which the Linn of Linn had promised them, the announcement had to do with the title of co-Lord Leader, which had been bestowed on him.

"I am sure," he told the crowd, "that you will agree with me that the title of Lord Leader belongs uniquely to the first and greatest man of Linn. I therefore request, and will hold it mandatory upon government leaders, that I be addressed as Lord Adviser. It shall be my pleasure to act as adviser to both the Lord Leader and the patronate, and it is in this role that I wish to be known henceforth to the people of the mighty Linnan empire. Thank you for listening to me, and I now advise you that there will be games for three days in the bowls, and that free food will be served throughout the city during that time at my expense. Go and have a good time, and may the gods of the atoms bring you all good luck."

During the first minute after he had finished, Lydia was appalled. Was Tews mad to have refused the title of Lord Leader? The joyful yelping of the mob soothed her a little, and then, slowly, as she followed Tews and the old man along the promenade that led from the rostrum to the palace gates, she began to realize the cleverness of the new title. Lord Adviser. Why, it would be a veritable shield against the charges of those who were always striving to rouse the people against the absolute government of the Linns. It was clear that the long exile had sharpened rather than dulled the mind of her son.

The Lord Leader, too, as the days passed and the new character of Tews came to the fore, was having regrets. Certain restrictions, which he had imposed upon his stepson during his residence on Awai, seemed unduly severe and ill-advised in retrospect. He should not, for instance, have permitted Tews' wife to divorce him but should have insisted instead that she accompany him.

It seemed to him now that there was only one solution. He rushed the marriage between Tews and Gudrun, and then dispatched them to Venus on their honeymoon, taking the precaution of sending a quarter of a million men along, so that the future Lord Leader could combine his love-making with war-making.

Having solved his main troubles, the Lord Leader gave himself up to the chore of aging gracefully and of thinking out ways and means whereby his other heirs might be spared from the death which the thoughtful Lydia was undoubtedly planning for them.

All too soon, despite his own and his physicians' precautions, the Lord Leader sank into his final illness. He lay in his bed of pillows sweating out his last hours. All the wiles of the palace physician—including an ice-cold bath, a favorite remedy of his—failed to rally the stricken great man. In a few hours, the patronate was informed, and state leaders were invited to officiate at the death bed. The Linn of Linn had some years before introduced a law that no ruler was ever to be allowed to die incommunicado.

It was a thoughtful precaution against poisoning which he had considered extremely astute at the time, but which now, as he watched the crowds surging outside the open doors of his bedroom, and listened to the subdued roar of voices, seemed somewhat less than dignified.

He motioned to Lydia. She came gliding over, and nodded at his request that the door be closed. Some of the people in the bedroom looked at each other, as she shooed them away, but the mild voice of the Lord Leader urged them, and so they trooped out. It took about ten minutes to clear the room. The Lord Leader lay, then, looking sadly up at his wife. He had an unpleasant duty to perform, and the unfortunate atmosphere of imminent death made the affair not less but more sordid. He began without preliminary.

"In recent years I have frequently hinted to you about fears I have had about the health of my relatives. Your reactions have left me no recourse but to doubt that you now have left in your heart any of the tender feelings which are supposed to be the common possession of womankind."

"What's this?" said Lydia. She had her first flash of insight as to what was coming. She said grimly, "My dear husband, have you gone out of your head?"

The Lord Leader continued calmly: "For once, Lydia, I am not going to speak in diplomatic language. Do not go through with your plans to have my relatives assassinated as soon as I am dead."

The language was too strong for the woman. The color deserted her cheeks, and she was suddenly as pale as lead. "I," she breathed, "kill your kin!"

The once steel-gray, now watery eyes stared at her with remorseless purpose. "I have put Jerrin and Draid beyond your reach. They are in command of powerful armies, and my will leaves explicit instructions about their future. Some of the men who are administrators, are likewise protected to some extent. The women are not so fortunate. My own two daughters are safe, I think. The elder is childless and without ambition, and Gudrun is now the wife of Tews. But I want a promise from you that you will not attempt to harm her, and that you will similarly refrain from taking any action against her three children, by her first marriage. I want your promise to include the children of my three cousins, and finally I want a promise from you about the Lady Tania, her two daughters, and her son, Lord Clane."

"Clane!" said Lydia. Her mind had started working as he talked. It leaped past the immense insult she was being offered, past all the names, to that one individual. She spoke the name again, more loudly.

"Clane!"

Her eyes were distorted pools. She glared at her husband with a bitter intensity. "And what," she said, "makes you think, who suspects me capable of such crimes, that I would keep such a promise to a dead man?"

The old man was suddenly less bleak. "Because, Lydia," he said quietly, "you are more than just a mother protecting

113

her young. You also are a leader whose political sagacity and general intelligence made possible the virtually united empire, which Tews will now inherit. You are at heart an honest woman, and if you made me a promise I think you would keep it."

She knew he was merely hoping now. And her calmness came back. She watched him with bright eyes, conscious of how weak was the power of a dying man, no matter how desperately he strove to fasten his desires and wishes upon his descendants.

"Very well, my old darling," she soothed him, "I will make you the promise you wish. I guarantee not to murder any of these people you have mentioned."

The Lord Leader gazed at her in despair. He had, he realized, not remotely touched her. This woman's basic integrity—and he knew it was there—could no longer be reached through her emotions. He abandoned that line immediately.

"Lydia," he said, "don't anger Clane by trying to kill him."

"Anger him!" said Lydia. She spoke sharply, because the phrase was so unexpected. She gazed at her husband with a startled wonder, as if she couldn't be quite sure that she had heard him correctly. She repeated the words slowly, listening to them as if she somehow might catch their secret meaning.

"Anger him?"

"You must realize," said the Lord Leader, "that you have some fifteen or twenty years of life to endure after my death, provided you hoard your physical energies. If you spend those years trying to run the world through Tews, you will quickly and quite properly be discarded by him. That is something which is not yet clear to you, and so I advise you to reorientate yourself. You must seek your power through other men. Jerrin will not need you, and Draid needs only Jerrin. Tews can and will dispense with you. That leaves Clane, of the great men. He can use you. Through him, therefore, you will be able to retain a measure of your power."

114

Her gaze was on his mouth every moment that he talked. She listened as his voice grew weaker, and finally trailed into nothingness. In the silence that fell between them, Lydia sat comprehending at last, so it seemed to her. This was Clane talking through his dying grandfather.

This was Clane's cunning appeal to the fears she might have for her own future. The Clane who had frustrated her designs on the slave girl, Selk, was now desperately striving to anticipate her designs on him.

Deep inside her, as she sat there watching the old man die, she laughed. Three months before, recognizing the signals of internal disintegration in her husband, she had insisted that Tews be recalled from Venus, and Jerrin appointed in his place. Her skill in timing was now bearing fruit, and it was working out even better than she had hoped. It would be at least a week before Tews' spaceship would arrive in Linn. During that week the widow Lydia would be all-powerful.

It was possible that she would have to abandon her plans against some of the other members of the family. But they at least were human. It was Clane, the alien, the creature, the nonhuman, who must be destroyed at any cost. She had one week in which she could, if necessary, use three whole legions and a hundred spaceships to smash him and the gods that had made him.

The long, tense conversation had dimmed the spark of life in the Lord Leader. Ten minutes before sunset, the great throngs outside saw the gates open, and Lydia leaning on the arms of two old patrons slowly walked out, followed by a crowd of noblemen. In a moment it was general knowledge that the Linn of Linn was dead.

13

Lydia wakened lazily on the morrow after the death of the Lord Leader. She stretched and yawned deliciously, reveling in the cool, clean sheets. Then she opened her eyes and stared at the ceiling. Bright sunlight was pouring through open windows, and Dalat hovered at the end of the bed. "You asked to be awakened early, honorable lady," she said.

There was a note of respect in her voice that Lydia had never noticed before. Her mind poised, pondering the imponderable difference. And then she got it. The Linn was dead. For one week she was not the legal but the *de facto* head of the city and state. None would dare oppose the mother of the new leader—uh, the Lord Adviser Tews. Glowing, Lydia sat up in bed. "Has there been any word yet from Meerl?"

"None, gracious lady."

She frowned over that. Her assassin had formed a relationship with her, which she had first accepted reluctantly, then, recognizing its value, with smiling grace. He had access to her bedroom at all hours of the day or night. And it was rather surprising that he to whom she had intrusted such an important errand, should not have reported long since.

Dalat was speaking again. "I think, madam, you should inform him, however, that it is unwise for him to have parcels delivered here addressed to himself in your care."

Lydia was climbing out of bed. She looked up, astounded and angry. "Why, the insolent fool, has he done that? Let me see the parcel."

She tore off the wrapping, furiously, and found herself staring down at a vase filled with ashes. A note was tied around the lip of the vase. Puzzled, she turned it over and read:

Dear Madam:
Your assassin was too moist. The atom gods, once roused, become frantic in the presence of moisture.

Uranium,
For the council of gods

CRASH! The sound of the vase smashing on the floor shocked her out of a blur of numbness. Wide-eyed she stared down at the little pile of ashes amid the broken pieces of pottery. With tense fingers she reached down, and picked up the note. This time, not the meaning of the note, but the signature, snatched at her attention: *Uranium.*

It was like a dash of cold water. With bleak eyes she gazed at the ashes of what had been Meerl, her most trustworthy assassin. She realized consciously that she felt this death more keenly than that of her husband. The old man had hung on too long. So long as life continued in his bones, he had the power to make changes. When he had finally breathed his last, she had breathed easily for the first time in years, as if a weight had been lifted from her soul.

But now, a new weight began to settle in its place, and her breath came in quick gasps. She kicked viciously at the ashes, as if she would shove the meaning of them out of her life. How could Meerl have failed? Meerl, the cautious, the skillful, Meerl the bold and brave and daring!

"Dalat!"

"Yes, lady?"

With narrowed eyes and pursed lips Lydia considered the action she was contemplating. But not for long. "Call Colonel Maljan. Tell him to come at once." She had one week to kill a man. And it was time to come out into the open.

Lydia had herself carried to the foot of the hill that led up to the estate of Lord Clane. She wore a heavy veil and used as carriers slaves who had never appeared with her in public, and an old unmarked chair of one of her ladies-in-waiting. Her eyes, that peered out of this excellent disguise, were bright with excitement.

The morning was unnaturally hot. Blasts of warm air came sweeping down the hill from the direction of Clane's house. And, after a little, she saw that the soldiers a hundred yards up the hill, had stopped. The pause grew long and puzzling, and she was just about to climb out of her chair, when she saw Maljan coming towards her. The dark-eyed, hawknosed officer was sweating visibly.

"Madam," he said, "we cannot get near that fence. It seems to be on fire."

"I can see no flame."

"It isn't that kind of a fire."

Lydia was amazed to see that the man was trembling with fright.

"There's something unnatural up there," he said. "I don't like it."

She came out of the chair then, the chill of defeat settling upon her. "Are you an idiot?" she snarled. "If you can't get past the fence, drop men from spaceships into the grounds."

"I've already sent for them," he said, "but—"

"*But!*" said Lydia, and it was a curse. "I'll go up and have a look at that fence myself."

She went up, and stopped short where the soldiers were gasping on the ground. The heat had already blasted at her, but at that point it took her breath away. She felt as if her lungs would sear inside her. In a moment her throat was ash dry. She stepped behind a bush. But it was no good. She saw that the leaves had seared and darkened. And then she was retreating behind a little knoblike depression in the hill. She crouched behind it, too appalled to think. She grew aware of Maljan working up towards her. He arrived, gasping, and it was several seconds before he could speak. Then he pointed up.

"The ships," he said.

She watched them creep in low over the trees. They listed a little as they crossed the fence, then sank out of sight and disappeared behind the trees that hid the meadow of Clane's estate. Five ships in all came into sight and disappeared over the rim of the estate. Lydia was keenly aware that their arrival relieved the soldiers sprawling helplessly all around her.

"Tell the men to get down the hill," she commanded hoarsely, and made the hastiest retreat of all. The street below was still almost deserted. A few people had paused to watch in a puzzled fashion the activities of the soldiers, but they moved on when commanded to do so by the guards who had been posted in the road. It was something to know that the campaign was still a private affair.

She waited. No sound came from beyond the trees where the ships had gone. It was as if they had fallen over some precipice into an abyss of silence. Half an hour went by, and then, abruptly, a ship came into sight. Lydia caught her breath, then watched the machine float towards them over the trees, and settle in the road below. A man in uniform came out. Maljan waved at him, and ran over to meet him. The conversation that followed was very earnest. At last Maljan turned, and with evident reluctance came towards her. He said in a low tone: "The house itself is offering an impregnable heat barrier. But they have talked to Lord Clane. He wants to speak to you."

She took that with a tense thoughtfulness. The realization had already penetrated deep that this stalemate might go on for days.

If I could get near him, she decided, remorselessly, *by pretending to consider his proposals*—

It seemed to work perfectly. By the time the spaceship lifted her over the fence, the heat that exuded from the walls of the house had died away to a bearable temperature. And, incredibly, Clane agreed that she could bring a dozen soldiers into the house as guards. As she entered, she had her first sense of eeriness. There was no one around, not a slave, not a movement of life. She headed in the direction of the bedroom, more slowly with each step. The first grudging admiration came. It seemed unbelievable that his preparations could have been so thorough as to include the evacuation of all his slaves. And yet it all fitted. Not once in her dealings with him had he made a mistake.

"Grandmother, I wouldn't come any closer."

She stopped short. She saw that she had come to within a yard of the corridor that led to his bedroom. Clane was standing at the far end, and he seemed to be quite alone and undefended.

"Come any nearer," he said, "and death will strike you automatically."

She could see nothing unusual. The corridor was much as she remembered it. The drapes had been taken down from the walls, revealing the temple stone underneath. And yet, standing there, she felt a faint warmth, unnatural and, suddenly, deadly. It was only with an effort that she threw off the feeling.

She parted her lips to give the command, but Clane spoke first.

"Grandmother, do nothing rash. Consider, before you defy the powers of the atom. Has what happened today not yet penetrated to your intelligence? Surely, you can see that whom the gods love no mortal can destroy."

The woman was bleak with her purpose. "You have misquoted the old saying," she said. "Whom the gods love die young."

And yet, once more, she hesitated. The stunning thing was that he continued to stand there less than thirty feet away, unarmed, unprotected, a faint smile on his lips. How far he has come, she thought. His nervous affliction, conquered now. And what a marvelously beautiful face, so calm, so confident.

Confident! Could it be that there *were* gods?

Could it be?

"Grandmother, I warn you, make no move. If you must prove that the gods will strike on my behalf, send your soldiers. *But do not move yourself.*"

She felt weak, her legs numb. The conviction that was pouring through her, the certainty that he was not bluffing brought a parallel realization that she could not back down. And yet she must.

She recognized that there was insanity in her terrible indecision. And knew, then, that she was not a person who was capable of conscious suicide. Therefore, quit, retreat, accept the reality of rout. She parted her lips to give the order to retire when it happened.

What motive impelled the soldier to action was never clear. Perhaps he grew impatient. Perhaps he felt there would be promotion for him. Whatever the reason, he suddenly cried out, "I'll get his gizzard for you!" And leaped forward. He went only a few feet past Lydia when he began to disintegrate. He crumpled like an empty sack. Where he had been, a mist of ashes floated lazily to the floor. There was one burst of heat, then. It came in a gust of unearthly hot wind, barely touched Lydia, who had instinctively jerked aside, but struck the soldiers behind her. There was a hideous masculine squealing and whimpering, followed by a mad scramble. A door slammed, and she was alone. She straightened, conscious that the air from the corridor was still blowing hot. She remained cautiously where she was, and called.

"Clane!"

The answer came instantly. "Yes, grandmother?"

For a moment, then, she hesitated, experiencing all the agony of a general about to surrender. At last, slowly, "What do you want?"

"An end to attacks on me. Full political co-operation, but people must remain unaware of it as long as we can possibly manage it."

"Oh!"

She began to breath easier. She had had a fear that he would demand public recognition.

"And if I don't?" she said at last.

"Death!"

It was quietly spoken. The woman did not even think to doubt. She was being given a chance. But there was one thing more. One tremendous thing more.

"Clane, is your ultimate goal the Lord Leadership?"

"No!"

His answer was too prompt. She felt a thrill of disbelief, a sick conviction that he was lying. But she was glad after a moment that he had denied. In a sense it bound him. Her thoughts soared to all the possibilities of the situation, then came down again to the sober necessity of this instant.

"Very well," she said, and it was little more than a sigh. "I accept."

Back at the palace, she sent an assassin to perform an essential operation against the one outsider who knew the Lady Lydia had suffered a major defeat. It was late afternoon when the double report came in. The exciting information that Tews had landed sooner than anticipated, and was even then on his way to the palace. And the satisfying words that Colonel Maljan lay dead in an alleyway with a knife in one of his kidneys.

It was only then that it struck her that she was now in the exact position that her dead husband had advised for her own safety and well-being.

Tears, and the realization of her great loss came as late as that.

On the tomb of the Lord Leader, the nation of Linn authorized a tribute never before given any man:

MEDRON LINN
FATHER OF THE EMPIRE

14

In high government and military circles in Linn and on Venus, the succession of battles with the Venusian tribesmen of the three central islands were called by their proper name: war! For propaganda purposes, the word, rebellion, was paraded at every opportunity. It was a necessary illusion. The enemy fought with the ferocity of a people who had tasted slavery. To rouse the soldiery to an equal pitch of anger and hatred there was nothing that quite matched the term, rebel.

Men who had faced hideous dangers in the swamps and marshes could scarcely restrain themselves at the thought that traitors to the empire were causing all the trouble. Lord Jerrin, an eminently fair man, who admired a bold and resourceful opponent, for once made no attempt to discourage the false impression. He recognized that the Linnans were the oppressors, and at times it made him physically ill that so many men must die to enforce a continued subjection. But he recognized, also, that there was no alternative.

The Venusians were the second most dangerous race in the solar system, second only to the Linnans. The two peoples had fought each other for three hundred and fifty years, and it was not until armies of Raheinl had landed on Uxta, the main island of Venus some forty years before that a victory of any proportions was scored. The young military genius was only eighteen at the time of the battle of the Casuna Marsh. Swift conquest of two other islands followed, but then his dazzled followers in Linn provoked the civil war that finally ended after nearly eight years in the execution of Raheinl by the Lord Leader. The latter proceeded with a cold ferocity to capture four more island strongholds of the Venusians. In each one he set up a separate government, revived old languages, suppressed the common language—and so strove to make the islanders think of themselves as separate peoples.

For years they seemed to be—and then, abruptly, in one organized uprising they seized the principal cities of the five main islands. And discovered that the Lord Leader had been more astute than they imagined. The military strongholds were not in the cities, as they had assumed, and as their spies had reported. The centers of Linnan power were located in an immense series of small forts located in the marshes. These forts had always seemed weak outposts, designed to discourage raiders rather than rebellions. And no Venusian had ever bothered to count the number of them. The showy city forts, which were elaborately attacked, turned out to be virtual hollow shells. By the time the Venusians rallied to attack the forts in the marshes it was too late for the surprise to be effective. Reinforcements were on the way from Earth. What had been planned as an all-conquering coup became a drawn-out war. And long ago, the awful empty feeling had come to the Venusians that they couldn't win.

Month after month the vise of steel weapons, backed by fleets of spaceships and smaller craft, tightened noticeably around the ever-narrowing areas which they controlled. Food was becoming more scarce, and a poor crop year was in prospect. The men were grim and tense, the women cried a great deal and made much of their children, who had caught the emotional overtones of the atmosphere of fear. Terror bred cruelty. Captive Linnans were hanged from posts, their feet dangling only a few inches from the ground. The distorted dead faces of the victims glared at the distorted hate-filled faces of their murderers. The living knew that each account would be paid in rape and death. They were exacting their own payments in advance.

The situation was actually much more involved than it appeared. Some six months before, the prospect of an imminent triumph for Jerrin had penetrated to the Lord Adviser Tews. He pondered the situation with a painful understanding of how the emotions of the crowd might be seduced by so momentous a victory. His own liberal plans, which he continued to tell himself that he cherished—though they had become vaguer—might be threatened. After considerable thought he resurrected a request from Jerrin for reinforcements, which had been made more than a year before. At the time Tews had considered it inexpedient to hasten the Venusian war to a quick end, but second thought brought an idea. With a pomp of public concern for Jerrin he presented the request to the patronate and added his urgent recommendations that at least three legions be assembled to assist "our hard-pressed forces against a skillful and cunning enemy."

He could have added, but didn't, that *he* intended to deliver the reinforcements and so participate in the victory. The patronate would not dare to refuse to vote him a triumph co-equal with that already being planned for Jerrin. He discussed his projected trip with his mother, the Lady Lydia, and, in accordance with her political agreement with Clane, she duly passed the information on to the mutation. Lydia had no sense of betraying her son. She had no such intention. But she knew that the fact that Tews was going to Venus would soon be common knowledge, and so, sardonically, she reported to Clane less than two weeks before Tews was due to leave.

His reaction startled her. The very next day he requested an audience with Tews. And the latter, who had adopted an affable manner with the late Lord Leader's grandchildren, did not think of refusing Clane's request for permission to organize an expedition to Venus.

He was surprised when the expedition departed within one week of the request, but he thought that over, also, and found it good. The presence of Clane on Venus would embarrass Jerrin. The birth of a mutation twenty-five years before into the ruling family of Linn had caused a sensation. His existence had dimmed the superstitions about such semihumans, but the fears of the ignorant were merely confused. Under the proper circumstances people would still stone them—and soldiers might become panicky at the thought of the bad luck that struck an army, the rank and file of which saw a mutation just before a battle.

He explained his thoughts to Lydia, adding, "It will give me a chance to discover whether Jerrin was implicated in any way in the three plots against me that I have put down in the past year. And if he were, I can make use of the presence of Clane."

Lydia said nothing, but the falseness of the logic disturbed her. She, also, had once planned against Clane. For months now, she had questioned the blind impulse of mother love that had made her conspire to bring Tews to power. Under Tews, the government creaked along indecisively while he writhed and twisted in a curious and ungraceful parody of modest pretense at establishing a more liberal government. His plans of transition were too vague. An old tactician herself, it seemed to her that she could recognize a developing hypocrite when she saw one.

"He's beginning to savor the sweetness of power," she thought, "and he realizes he's talked too much."

The possibilities made her uneasy. It was natural for a politician to fool others, but there was something ugly and dangerous about a politician who fooled himself. Fortunately, little that was dangerous could happen on Venus. Her own investigations had convinced her that the conspiracies against Tews had involved no important families, and besides Jerrin was not a man who would force political issues. He would be irritated by the arrival of Tews. He would see exactly what Tews wanted, but he would do nothing about it.

After the departure of Tews and his three legions, she settled herself to the routine task of governing for him. She had a number of ideas for re-establishing firmer control over the patronate, and there were about a hundred people whom she had wanted to kill for quite a long while.

During the entire period of the crisis on Venus, life in Linn went on with absolute normalcy.

15

At first the land below was a shadow seen through mist. As the three spaceships of Lord Clane Linn's expedition settled through the two thousand mile atmosphere, the blurriness went out of the scene. Mountains looking like maps rather than territories took form. The vast sea to the north sank beyond the far horizon of swamps and marshes, hills and forests. The reality grew wilder and wilder, but the pit was directly ahead now, an enormous black hole in the long narrow plain.

The ships settled to the ground on a green meadow half a mile from the nearest edge of the pit, which lay to the northeast. Some six hundred men and women, three hundred of them slaves, emerged from the vessels, and a vast amount of equipment was unloaded. By nightfall habitations had been erected for Clane and the three slave women who attended him, for two knights and three temple scientists and five scholars not connected with a religious organization. In addition, a corral had been built for the slaves, and the two companies of soldiers were encamped in a half circle around the main camp.

Sentries were posted, and the spaceships withdrew to a height of about five hundred feet. All night long, a score of fires, tended by trusted slaves, brightened the darkness. Dawn came uneventfully, and slowly the camp took up the activities of a new day. Clane did not remain to direct it. Immediately after breakfast, horses were saddled; and he and twenty-five men, including a dozen armed soldiers, set out for the nearby home of the gods.

They were all rank unbelievers, but they had proceeded only a few hundred yards when Clane noticed that one of the riders was very pale. He reined up beside him.

"Breakfast upset you?" he asked gently. "Better go back to camp and rest today."

Most of those who were destined to continue watched the lucky man trot off out of sight into the brush.

The evenness of the land began to break. Gashes opened in the earth at their feet, and ran off at a slant towards the pit, which was still not visible beyond the trees. Straight were those gashes, too straight, as if long ago irresistible objects had hurtled up out of the pit each at a different angle, each tearing the intervening earth as it darted up out of the hell below.

Clane had a theory about the pits. Atomic warfare by an immeasurably superior civilization. Atomic bombs that set up a reaction in the ground where they landed, and only gradually wore themselves out in the resisting soil, concrete and steel of vast cities. For centuries the remnants roiled and flared with deadly activity. How long? No one knew. He had an idea that if star maps of the period could be located an estimate of the time gap might be possible. The period involved must be very great, for several men that he knew had visited pits on Earth without ill effects.

The god fires were dying down. It was time for intellectually bold men to begin exploring. Those who came first would find the treasures. Most of the pits on Earth were absolutely barren affairs overgrown with weeds and brush. A few showed structures in their depths, half buried buildings, tattered walls, mysterious caverns. Into these a handful of men had ventured—and brought back odd mechanical creations, some obviously wrecks, a few that actually worked: all tantalizing in their suggestion of a science marvelous beyond anything known to the temple scholars. It was this pit on Venus, which they were now approaching, that had always excited the imagination of the adventurers. For years visitors had crouched behind lead or concrete barriers and peered with periscopes into the fantastic depths below.

The nameless city that had been there must have been built into the bowels of the earth. For the bottom was a mass of concrete embankments, honeycombed with black holes that seemed to lead down into remoter depths.

Clane's reverie died down. A soldier in front of him let out a shout, reined in his horse and pointed ahead. Clane urged his horse up to the rise on top of which the man had halted. And reined in *his* horse. He was looking down a gently sloping grassy embankment. It ran along for about a hundred feet. And then there was a low concrete wall.

Beyond was the pit.

At first they were careful. They used the shelter of the wall as a barrier to any radiation that might be coming up from below. Clane was the exception. From the beginning he stood upright, and peered downward through his glasses into the vista of distance below. Slowly the others lost their caution, and finally all except two artists were standing boldly on their feet gazing into the most famous home of the gods.

It was not a clear morning. A faint mist crawled along hiding most of the bottom of the pit. But it was possible, with the aid of the glasses, to make out contours, and to see the far precipice nearly seven miles away.

About midmorning, the mists cleared noticeably, and the great sun of Venus shone down into the hole, picking out every detail not hidden by distance. The artists, who had already sketched the main outlines, settled down to work in earnest. They had been selected for their ability to draw maps, and the watchful Clane saw that they were doing a good job. His own patience, product of his isolated upbringing, was even greater than theirs. All through that day he examined the bottom of the pit with his glasses, and compared the reality with the developing drawings on the drawing boards.

By late afternoon the job was complete, and the results very satisfactory. There were no less than three routes for getting out of the pit on foot in case of an emergency. And every tree and cave opening below was clearly marked in its relation to other trees and openings. Lines of shrubs were sketched in, and each map was drawn to scale.

That night, also, passed without incident. The following morning Clane signaled one of the spaceships to come down, and, shortly after breakfast, the two temple scientists, one knight, three artists, a dozen soldiers, a crew of fifteen and he climbed aboard. The ship floated lightly clear of the ground. And, a few minutes later, nosed over the edge of the pit, and headed downward.

They made no attempt to land, but simply cruised around searching for radioactive areas. Round and round at a height that varied between five hundred feet and a daring two hundred feet. It *was* daring. The spaceship was their sole instrument for detecting the presence of atomic energy. Long ago, it had been discovered that when a spaceship passed directly above another spaceship, the one that was on top suffered a severe curtailment of its motive power. Immediately it would start to fall. In the case of spaceships, the two ships would usually be moving so swiftly that they would be past each other almost immediately. Quickly, then, the disabled ship would right itself and proceed on its way.

Several attempts had been made by military scientists to utilize the method to bring down enemy spaceships. The attempts, however, were strictly limited by the fact that a ship which remained five hundred feet above the source of energy endured so slight a hindrance that it didn't matter.

Nine times their ship made the tell-tale dip, and then, for as long as was necessary they would cruise over and over the area trying to define its limits, locating it on their maps, marking off first the danger zone, then the twilight zone and finally the safety zone. The final measure was the strength or weakness of the impulse. The day ended, with that phase of their work still uncompleted. And it was not until noon the next day that the details were finally finished. Since it was too late to make a landing, they returned to camp and spent the afternoon sleeping off their accumulated fatigue.

It was decided that the first landing would be made by one hundred men, and that they would take with them supplies for two weeks. The site of the landing was selected by Clane after consultation with the knights and the scientists. From the air, it appeared to be a large concrete structure with roof and walls still intact, but its main feature was that it was located near one of the routes by which the people on foot could leave the pit. And it was surrounded by more than a score of the cavelike openings.

The spaceship came down without incident, and the air lock was opened immediately. Stepping to the edge of the door, Clane had an impression of intense silence. He lowered himself over the edge, and for the first time stood on ground that, until now, he had seen only from a distance. The other men began to scramble down after him, and there was a pleasurable sound of activity, breaking the stillness. The morning air quickly echoed to the uproar of a hundred men breathing, walking, moving—and unloading supplies.

Less than an hour after he first set foot into the soft soil of the pit, Clane watched the spaceship lift from the ground, and climb rapidly up about five hundred feet. At that height it leveled off, and began its watchful cruise back and forth above the explorers.

Once again no hasty moves were made. Tents were set up and a rough defense marked off. The food was sealed off behind a pile of concrete. Shortly before noon, after an early lunch, Clane, one knight, one temple scientist and six soldiers left the encampment and walked toward the "building" which, among other things, had attracted them to the area. Seen from this near vantage point it was not a building at all, but an upjutment of concrete and metal, a remnant of what had once been a man-made burrow into depths of the earth, a monument to the futility of seeking safety by mechanical rather than intellectual and moral means. The sight of it depressed Clane. For a millennium it had stood here, first in a seething ocean of unsettled energy, and now amid a great silence it waited for the return of man.

His own estimate of the time that had gone by since the great war was of the order of 8,000 years. He had enough data from other pits concerning the calendar system of the ancients to guess that by their reckoning, present-day Linn was existing in 12,000 A.D.

He paused to examine a partly open door, then motioned two soldiers to push at it. They were unable to budge it, and so, waving them aside, he edged gingerly past the rusted door jamb. He found himself in a narrow hallway, which ran along for about eight feet, and then there was another door. A closed door this time. The floor was concrete, the walls and ceiling concrete, but the door was metal. Clane and the knight, a big man with black eyes, shoved it open with scarcely an effort, though it creaked rustily as they did.

They stood there, startled. The interior was not dark as they expected, but dimly lighted. The luminous glow came from a series of small bulbs in the ceiling. The bulbs were not transparent, but coated with an opaque coppery substance. The light shone through the coating. Nothing like it had ever been seen in Linn or elsewhere. After a blank period, Clane wondered if the lights had turned on when they opened the door. They discussed it briefly, then shut the door. Nothing happened. They opened the door again, but the lights did not even flicker. They had obviously been burning for centuries.

With a genuine effort, he suppressed the impulse to have the treasures taken down immediately and carried to the camp.

The deathly silence, the air of immense antiquity brought the same realization that there was no necessity to act swiftly here. He was first on this scene. Slowly, almost reluctantly, he turned his attention from the ceiling to the room itself. A wrecked table stood in one corner. In front of it was a chair with one leg broken and a single strand of wood where the seat had been. In the adjoining corner was a pile of rubble, including a skull and some vaguely recognizable ribs which merged into a powdery skeleton. The relic of what had once been a human being lay on top of a rather long, all-metal rod. There was

132

nothing else in the room. Clane strode forward and eased the rod from under the skeleton. The movement, slight though it was, was too much for the bone structure. The skull and ribs dissolved into powder, and faint white mist hovered for a moment, then settled to the floor. He stepped back gingerly, and, still holding the rod, passed through the door, and along the narrow hallway, and so out into the open.

The outside scene was different. He had been gone from it fifteen minutes at most, but in that interval a change had taken place. The spaceship that had brought them was still cruising around overhead. But a second spaceship was in the act of settling down beside the camp.

It squashed down with a crackling of brush and an "harumph" sound of air squeezing out from the indentation it made in the ground. The door opened, and, as Clane headed for the camp, three men emerged from it. One wore the uniform of an aid-de-camp to supreme head-quarters, and it was he who handed Clane a dispatch pouch. The pouch contained a single letter from his eldest brother, Lord Jerrin, General-in-Chief of Linnan armies on Venus. In the will of the late Lord Leader, Jerrin had been designated to become co-ruler with Tews when he attained the age of thirty, his sphere of administration to be the planets. His powers in Linn were to be strictly secondary to those of Tews. His letter was curt:

It has come to my attention that you have arrived on Venus. I need hardly point out to you that the presence of a mutation here at this critical period of the war against the rebels is bound to have an adverse effect. I have been told that your request for this trip was personally granted by the Lord Adviser Tews. If you are not aware of the intricate motives that might inspire Tews to grant such permission, then you are not alert to the possible disasters that might befall our branch of the family. It is my wish and command that you return to Earth at once.

Jerrin

133

As Clane looked up from the letter, he saw that the commander of the spaceship which had brought the messenger, was silently signaling to him. He walked over and drew the captain aside.

"I didn't want to worry you," the man said, "but perhaps I had better inform you that this morning, shortly after your expedition entered the pit, we saw a very large body of men riding along several miles to the northwest of the pit. They have shown no inclination to move in this direction, but they scattered when we swooped over them, which means that they are Venusian rebels."

Clane stood frowning for a moment, then nodded his acceptance of the information. He turned away, into his spacious tent, to write an answer to his brother that would hold off the crisis between *them* until the greater crisis that had brought him to Venus shattered Jerrin's disapproval of his presence.

That crisis was due to break over Jerrin's unsuspecting head in just about one week.

16

Tews took up his quarters in the palace of the long-dead Venusian emperor, Heerkel, across town from the military headquarters of Jerrin. It was an error of the kind that startles and starts history. The endless parade of generals and other officers that streamed in and out of Mered passed him by. A few astute individuals made a point of taking the long journey across the city, but even some of these were in obvious haste, and could scarcely tolerate the slow ceremoniousness of an interview with their ruler.

A great war was being fought. Officers in from the front line took it for granted that their attitude would be understood. They felt remote from the peaceful pomp of Linn itself. Only the men who had occasion to make trips to Earth comprehended the vast indifference of the population to the war on Venus. To the people at home it was a faraway frontier affair. Such engagements had been fought continuously from the time of their childhood, only every once in a while the scene changed.

His virtual isolation sharpened the suspicions with which Tews had landed. And frightened him. He hadn't realized how widespread was the disaffection. The plot must be well advanced, so advanced that thousands of officers knew about it, and were taking no chances on being caught with the man who, they must have decided, would be the loser. They probably looked around them at the enormous armies under the command of Jerrin. And knew that no one could defeat the man who had achieved the loyalty of so many legions of superb soldiers.

Swift, decisive action, it seemed to Tews, was essential. When Jerrin paid him a formal visit a week after his arrival, he was startled at the cold way in which Tews rejected his request that the reinforcements be sent to the front for a final smashing drive against the marsh-bound armies of the Venusians.

"And what," said Tews, noting with satisfaction the other's disconcertment, "would you do should you gain the victory which you anticipate?"

The subject of the question, rather than the tone, encouraged the startled Jerrin. He had had many thoughts about the shape of the coming victory, and after a moment he decided that that was actually why Tews had come to Venus, to discuss the political aspects of conquest. The older man's manner he decided to attribute to Tews' assumption of power. This was the new leader's way of reacting to his high position.

Briefly, Jerrin outlined his ideas. Execution of certain leaders directly responsible for the policy of murdering

135

prisoners, enslavement only of those men who had participated intimately in the carrying out of the executions. But all the rest to be allowed to live without molestation, and in fact to return to their homes in a normal fashion. At first each island would be administered as a separate colony, but even during the first phase the common language would be restored and free trade permitted among the islands. The second phase, to begin in about five years, and widely publicized in advance, should be the establishment of responsible government on the separate islands, but those governments would be part of the empire, and would support the occupation troops. The third phase should start ten years after that, and would include the organization of one central all-Venusian administration for the islands, with a federal system of government.

And this system, also, would have no troops of its own, and would be organized entirely within the framework of the empire.

Five years later, the fourth and final phase could begin. All families with a twenty-year record of achievement and loyalty could apply for Linnan-Venusian citizenship, with all the privileges and opportunities for self-advancement that went with it.

"It is sometimes forgotten," said Jerrin, "that Linn began as a city-state, which conquered neighboring cities, and held its power in them by a gradual extension of citizenship. There is no reason why this system should not be extended to the planets with equal success." He finished, "All around us is proof that the system of absolute subjection employed during the past fifty years had been a complete failure. The time has come for new and more progressive statesmanship."

Tews almost stood up in his agitation, as he listened to the scheme. He could see the whole picture now. The late Lord Leader had in effect willed the planets to Jerrin; and this was Jerrin's plan for welding his inheritance into a powerful military stronghold, capable, if necessary, of conquering Linn itself.

Tews smiled a cold smile. *Not yet, Jerrin,* he thought,

I'm still absolute ruler, and for three years what I say is what will happen. Besides, your plan might interfere with my determination to re-establish the republic at an opportune moment. I'm pretty sure that you, with all your liberalistic talk, have no intention of restoring constitutional government. It is that ideal that must be maintained at all costs.

Aloud, he said, "I will take your recommendations under advisement. But now, it is my wish that in future all promotions be channeled through me. Any commands that you issue to commanding officers in the field are to be sent here for my perusal, and I will send them on." He finished with finality, "The reason for this is that I wish to familiarize myself with the present positions of all units and with the names of the men in charge of them. That is all. It has been a privilege to have had this conversation with you. Good day, sir."

Move number one was as drastic as that. It was only the beginning. As the orders and documents began to arrive, Tews studied them with the assiduity of a clerk. His mind reveled in paper work, and the excitement of his purpose made every detail important and interesting. He knew this Venusian war. For two years he had sat in a palace some hundred miles farther back, and acted the role of commander-in-chief, now filled by Jerrin. His problem, therefore, did not include the necessity of learning the situation from the beginning. He had merely to familiarize himself with the developments during the past year and a half. And, while numerous, they were not insurmountable.

From the first day, he was able to accomplish his primary purpose: replacement of doubtful officers with one after another of the horde of sycophants he had brought with him from Linn. Tews felt an occasional twinge of shame at the device, but he justified it on the grounds of necessity. A man contending with conspiring generals must take recourse to devious means. The important thing was to make sure that the army was not used against himself, the Lord Adviser, the lawful heir of Linn, the only man whose ultimate purposes were not autocratic and selfish.

As a secondary precaution, he altered several of Jerrin's troop dispositions. These had to do with legions that Jerrin had brought with him from Mars, and which presumably might be especially loyal to him personally. It would be just as well if he didn't know their exact location during the next few critical weeks.

On the twelfth day he received from a spy the information for which he had been waiting. Jerrin, who had gone to the front on an inspection tour two days before, was returning to Mered. Tews actually had only an hour's warning. He was still setting the stage for the anticipated interview when Jerrin was announced. Tews smiled at the assembled courtiers.

He said in a loud voice, "Inform his excellency that I am engaged at the moment but that if he will wait a little I shall be happy to receive him."

The remark, together with the knowing smile that went with it, started a flutter of sensation through the room. It was unfortunate that Jerrin had failed to wait for his message to be delivered, but was already halfway across the room. He did not pause until he was standing in front of Tews. The latter regarded him with indolent insolence.

"Well, what is it?"

Jerrin said quietly, "It is my unpleasant duty, my Lord Adviser, to inform you that it will be necessary to evacuate all civilians from Mered without delay. As a result of rank carelessness on the part of certain front-line officers, the Venusians have achieved a breakthrough north of the city. There will be fighting in Mered before morning."

Some of the ladies, and not a few of the gentlemen who were present uttered alarmed noises, and there was a general movement towards exits. A bellow from Tews stopped the disgraceful stampede. He settled heavily back in his chair and smiled a twisted smile.

"I hope," he said, "that the negligent officers have been properly punished."

"Thirty-seven of them," said Jerrin, "have been executed.

138

Here is a list of their names, which you might examine at your leisure.

Tews sat up. "Executed!" He had a sudden awful suspicion that Jerrin would not lightly have executed men who had long been under his command. With a jerk he tore the seal from the document and glanced rapidly down the column. Every name on it was that of one of his satellite-replacements of the past twelve days.

Very slowly he raised his eyes, and stared at the younger man. Their gaze met and held. The flinty blue eyes of Tews glared with an awful rage. The steel gray eyes of Jerrin were remorseless with contempt and disgust. "Your most gracious excellency," he said in a soft voice, "one of my Martian legions has been cut to pieces. The carefully built-up strategy and envelopment of the past year is wiped out. It is my opinion that the men responsible for that had better get off Venus, and back to their pleasures in Linn— or what they feared so foolishly will really transpire."

He realized immediately it was a wild statement. His words stiffened Tews. For a moment the big man's heavy face was a mask of tensed anger, then with a terrible effort he suppressed his fury. He straightened.

"In view of the seriousness of the situation," he said, "I will remain in Mered and take charge of the forces on this front until further notice. You will surrender your headquarters to my officers immediately."

"If your officers," said Jerrin, "come to my headquarters, they will be whipped into the streets. And that applies to *anyone* from this section of the city."

He turned and walked out of the room. He had no clear idea as to what he was going to do about the fantastic crisis that had arisen.

17

Clane spent those three weeks, when the Venusian front was collapsing, exploring a myriad of holes in the pit. And, although the threat from the wandering parties of Venusians did not materialize, he moved his entire party into the pit for safety. Guards were posted at the three main routes leading down into the abyss, and two spaceships maintained a continuous vigil over the countryside around the pit, and over the pit itself. These precautions were not a complete guarantee of safety, but they added up fairly well. Any attempt of a large body of troops to come down and attack the camp would be such an involved affair that there would be plenty of time to embark everyone on spaceships, and depart.

It was not the only thing in their favor. After a half century under Linnan rule, and though they themselves worshiped a sea god called Submerne, the Venusians respected the Linnan atom gods. It was doubtful if they would risk divine displeasure by penetrating into one of the pit homes of the gods. And so the six hundred people in the pit were cut off from the universe by barriers of the mind as well as by the sheer inaccessibility of the pit. Yet they were not isolated.

Daily one of the spaceships made the trip to Mered, and when it returned to the depths of the pit Clane would go aboard and knock on door after door. Each time he would be cautiously admitted by a man or a woman, and the two would hold a private conference. His spies never saw each other. They were always returned to Mered at dusk, and landed one by one in various parts of the city.

The spies were not all mercenaries. There were men in the highest walks of the empire who regarded the Linn mutation as the logical heir of the late Lord Leader. To them Tews was merely a stopgap who could be put out of the way at the proper time. Again and again, such individuals, who belonged to other groups, had secretly turncoated after meeting Clane, and become valuable sources of information for him. Clane knew his situation better than his well-wishers. However much he might impress intelligent people, the fact was that a mutation could not become ruler of the empire. Long ago, accordingly, he had abandoned some early ambitions in that direction, retaining only two main political purposes.

He was alive and in a position of advantage because his family was one of the power groups in Linn. Though he had no friends among his own kin, he was tolerated by them because of the blood relationship. It was to his interest that they remained in high position. In crises he must do everything possible to help them. That was purpose number one.

Purpose number two was to participate in some way in all the major political moves made in the Linnan empire, and it was rooted in an ambition that he could never hope to realize. He wanted to be a general. War in its practical aspects, as he had observed it from afar, seemed to him crude and unintelligent. From early childhood he had studied battle strategy and tactics with the intention of reducing the confusion to a point where battles could be won by little more than irresistible maneuver.

He arrived in Mered on the day following the clash between Tews and Jerrin, and took up residence in a house which he had long ago thoughtfully reserved for himself and his retinue. He made the move as unobtrusively as possible, but he did not delude himself that his coming would be unremarked. Other men, also, were diabolically clever. Other men maintained armies of spies as he did. All plans that depended upon secrecy possessed the fatal flaw of fragility. And the fact that they sometimes succeeded merely proved that a given victim was not himself an able man. It was one of the pleasures of life to be able to make all the preparations necessary to an enterprise within the sight and hearing of one's opponent.

Without haste he set about making them.

18

When Tews was first informed of Clane's arrival in Mered, about an hour after the event, his interest was dim. More important—or so they seemed—reports were arriving steadily from other sources about the troop dispositions Jerrin was making for the defense of the city. What puzzled Tews was that some of the information came from Jerrin in the form of copies of the orders he was sending out.

Was the man trying to re-establish relations by ignoring the fact that a break had taken place? It was an unexpected maneuver, and it could only mean that the crisis had come before Jerrin was ready. Tews smiled coldly as he arrived at the conclusion. His prompt action had thrown the opposition into confusion. It should not be difficult to seize Jerrin's headquarters the following morning with his three legions, and so end the mutiny.

By three o'clock Tews had sent out the necessary orders. At four, a very special spy of his, the impoverished son of a knight, reported that Clane had sent a messenger to Jerrin, requesting an interview that evening. Almost simultaneously other spies reported on the activity that was taking place at Clane's residence. Among other things several small round objects wrapped in canvas were brought from the spaceship into the house. More than a ton of finely ground copper dust was carried in sacks into a concrete outhouse. And finally a cube of material of the type used to build temples was carefully lowered to the ground. It must have been hot as well as heavy, because the slaves who took it into the house used slings and leadlined asbestos gloves.

Tews pondered the facts, and the very meaninglessness of them alarmed him. He suddenly remembered vague stories he had heard about the mutation, stories to which he had hitherto paid no attention. It was not a moment to take chances. Ordering a guard of fifty men to attend him, he set out for Clane's Mered home.

His first sight of the place startled Tews. The spaceship which, according to his reports, had flown away, was back. Suspended from a thick cable attached to its lower beam was a large gondola of the type slung under spaceships when additional soldiers were to be transported swiftly. They were used in space to carry freight only. Now, it lay on the ground and slaves swarmed over it. Not until he was on the estate itself did Tews see what they were doing.

Each man had a canvas bag of copper dust suspended around his neck, and some kind of liquid chemical was being used to work the copper dust into the semi-transparent hull of the carrier.

Tews climbed out of his chair, a big, plump man with piercing blue eyes. He walked slowly around the gondola, and the longer he looked the more senseless was the proceeding. And, oddly, nobody paid the slightest attention to him. There were two guards, but they seemed to have received no instruction about spectators. They lounged in various positions, smoking, exchanging coarse jests, and otherwise quite unaware that the Lord Adviser of Linn was in their midst.

Tews did not enlighten them. He was puzzled and undecided, as he walked slowly towards the house. Again, no effort was made to interfere with his passage. In the large inner hallway, several temple scientists were talking and laughing. They glanced at him curiously but it did not seem to occur to them that he did not belong.

Tews said softly, "Is Lord Clane inside?"

143

One of the scientists half turned, then nodded over his shoulder, casually. "You'll find him in the den working on the benediction."

There were more scientists in the living room. Tews frowned inwardly as he saw them. He had come prepared for drastic action, if necessary. But it would be indiscreet to arrest Clane with so many temple scientists as witnesses. Besides, there were too many guards.

Not that he could imagine any reason for an arrest. This looked like a religious ceremony, being readied here. He found Clane in the den, a medium sized room leading onto a patio. Clane's back was to him, and he was bending intently over a cube of temple building material. Tews recognized it from the description his spies had given him as the "hot" heavy object that the sweating slaves had handled so carefully in transporting it from the spaceship. On the table near the "cube" were six half balls of coppery substance. He didn't have time to look at them closely, for Clane turned to see who had come in. He straightened with a smile.

Tews stood, looking questioningly at Clane. The younger man came over. "We are all hoping," he said, "that this rod, which we found in the pit of the gods, is the legendary rod of fire. According to the legend, a basic requirement was that the wielder be pure in heart, and that, if he were, the gods would at their own discretion, but under certain circumstances, activate the rod."

Tews nodded soberly, and motioned with his hand toward the object.

"It is with pleasure," he said, "that I find you taking these interests in religious matters. I think it important that a member of our illustrious family has attained high rank in the temples, and I wish to make clear that no matter what happens"—he paused significantly—"*no matter what happens* you may count on me as your protector and friend."

He returned to Heerkel's palace, but, being a careful, thoughtful man, who knew all too well that other people were not always as pure in heart as they pretended, he left his spies to watch out for possible subversive activity.

He learned in due course that Clane had been invited for dinner by Jerrin, but had been received with that cold formality which had long distinguished the relationship between the two brothers. One of the slave waiters, bribed by a spy, reported that once, during the meal, Clane urged that a hundred spaceships be withdrawn from patrols and assigned to some task which was not clear to the slave.

There was something else about opening up the battle lines to the northeast, but this was so vague that the Lord Adviser did not think of it again until, shortly after midnight, he was roused from sleep by the desperate cries of men, and the clash of metal outside his bedroom.

Before he could more than sit up, the door burst open, and swarms of Venusian soldiers poured inside.

The battle lines to the northeast had been opened up.

It was the third night of his captivity, the hanging night. Tews quivered as the guards came for him about an hour after dusk and led him out into the fire-lit darkness. He was to be the first. As his body swung aloft, twenty thousand Venusians would tug on the ropes around the necks of ten thousand Linnan soldiers. The writhings and twistings that would follow were expected to last ten or more minutes.

The night upon which Tews gazed with glazed eyes was like nothing he had ever seen. Uncountably numerous fires burned on a vast plain. In the near distance he could see the great post upon which he was to be executed. The other posts began just beyond it. There were rows of them, and they had been set up less than five feet apart, with the rows ten from each other, to make room for camp fires that lighted the scene.

The doomed men were already at their posts, tied hand and foot, the ropes around their necks. Tews could only see the first row with any clearness. They were all officers, that first line of victims; and they stood at ease almost to a man. Some were chatting with those near them, as Tews was led up, but the conversation stopped as they saw him.

Never in his life had Tews seen such consternation flare into so many faces at once. There were cries of horror, groans of incredulous despair. Tews had not expected to be recognized, but it was possible the men had been taunted with his identity. Actually, his three-day beard and the night with its flickering fire shadows gave them little opportunity to be sure. No one said anything as he mounted the scaffold. Tews himself stood stiff and pale as the rope was fitted around his neck. He had ordered many a man to be hanged in his time. It was a different and thrilling sensation to be the victim and not the judge.

The passion of anger that came was rooted in a comprehension that he wouldn't be where he was if he had actually believed that a reversal was in progress. Instead, he had *counted* on Jerrin maintaining his forces against the enemy, while his three legions seized control from Jerrin.

Deep down inside, he had believed in Jerrin's honesty. He had sought to humiliate him, so that he could nullify the rightful honors of a young man with whom he did not wish to share the power of the state. His desperate fury grew out of the rapidly materializing belief that Jerrin had in reality been plotting against him. That chaos of thought would have raged on but for one thing: At that moment he happened to glance down, and there, below the platform, with a group of Venusian leaders, stood Clane.

The shock was too great to take all in one mental jump. Tews glared down at the slim young man, and the picture was obviously clear now. There had been a treasonable deal between Jerrin and the Venusians. He saw that the mutation was in his temple scientist fatigue gown, and that he carried the four foot metal "rod of fire." That brought a memory. He had forgotten all about the benediction in the sky. He looked up, but the blackness was unrelieved. If the ship and the gondola were up there they were part of the night, invisible and unattainable.

He glanced down again at the mutation and braced himself to speak, but before he could say anything, Clane said, "Your

146

excellency, let us waste no time with recriminations. Your death would renew the civil war in Linn. That is the last thing we desire, as we shall prove tonight, beyond all your suspicious."

Tews had hold of himself now. With quick logic, he examined the chances of a rescue. There was none. If spaceships should try to land troops, the Venusians need merely pull on their ropes, and hang the bound men—and then turn their vast, assembled army to hold off the scattered attacks launched from scores of spaceships. That was one maneuver they had undoubtedly prepared against; and since it was the only possible hope, and *it* couldn't take place, then Clane's words were a fraud.

His thoughts were brought to an abrupt halt, for the Venusian emperor, a grim-faced man of fifty, was climbing the platform steps. He stood there for minutes while silence gradually fell on the enormous crowd. Then he stepped to the front group of megaphones and spoke in the common language of Venus.

"Fellow Venusians," he said, "on this night of our vengeance for all the crimes that have been committed against us by the empire of Linn, we have with us an agent of the commanding general of our vile enemy. He has come to us with an offer, and I want him to come up here and tell it to you, so that you can laugh in his face as I did."

There was a mass shriek from the darkness: "Hang him! Hang him, too!"

Tews was chilled by that fierce cry, but he was forced to admire the cunning of the Venusian leader. Here was a man whose followers must many times have doubted his wisdom in fighting. His face showed the savage lines of obstinacy, of a badly worried general, who knew what criticism could be. What an opportunity this was for gaining public support.

Clane was climbing the steps. He waited until silence once more was restored, and then said in a surprisingly strong voice: "The atom gods of Linn, whose agent I am, are weary of this war. I call upon them to end it NOW!"

The Venusian emperor started towards him. "That isn't what you were going to say," he cried. "You—" He stopped. Because the sun came out.

The sun came out. Several hours had passed since it had sunk behind the flaming horizon of the northern sea. Now, in one leap it had jumped to the sky directly overhead.

The scene of so many imminent deaths stood out as in the brightness of noon. All the posts with their victims still standing beneath them, the hundreds of thousands of Venusian spectators, the great plain with the now visible coastal city in the distance—were brilliantly lighted.

The shadows began on the other side of the plain. The city could only be seen by vague light reflections. The sea beyond to the north and the mountains to the south were as deep as ever in blackness.

Seeing that darkness, Tews realized that it was not the sun at all above, but an incredible ball of fire, a source of light that, in this cubic mile of space, equaled the sun in magnitude of light. The gods of Linn had answered the call made to them.

His realization ended. There was a cry from scores of thousands of throats, a cry stranger and more horrible than any sound that Tews had ever heard. There was fear in it, and despair, and an awful reverence. Men and women alike started to sink to their knees. At that moment the extent of the defeat that was here penetrated to the Venusian leader. He let out a terrible cry of his own—and leaped towards the catch that would release the trapdoor on which Tews stood. From the corner of one eye, Tews saw Clane bring up the rod of fire.

There was no fire but the emperor dissolved. Tews could never afterwards decide what actually happened, yet he had a persistent memory of a human being literally turning into liquid stuff. Liquid that collapsed onto the platform, and burned a hole through the wood. The picture was so impossible that he closed his eyes, and never again quite admitted the reality to himself. When he finally opened his eyes, spaceships were coming down from the sky. To the

148

now prostrate Venusians, the sudden appearance of fifty thousand Linnan soldiers among them must have seemed like a miracle as great as the two they had already witnessed.

An entire reserve army was captured that night, and though the war on other islands dragged on and on, the great island of Uxta was completely captured within a few weeks. Clane's words had been proved beyond all suspicions.

On a cloudy afternoon a week later, Clane was among the distinguished Linnans who attended the departure of the flotilla of ships which was to accompany the Lord Adviser Tews back to Earth. Tews and his retinue arrived, and as he came up to the platform, a group of temple initiates burst into a paroxysm of singing. The Lord Adviser stopped, and stood for a minute, a faint smile on his face, listening.

The return to Earth, quietly suggested by Clane, suited him completely. He would take with him the first tidings of the Venusian victory. He would have time to scotch any rumors that the Lord Adviser himself had been humiliatingly captured. And above all, he would be the one who would insist upon full triumph honors for Jerrin.

He was amazed that he had temporarily forgotten his old cunnings about things like that. As he climbed aboard the flagship, the initiates broke into a new spasm of sound.

It was clear that the atom gods, also, were satisfied.

19

In his initial address to the Patronate, following his return from Venus, Tews said among other things: "It is difficult for us to realize, but Linn is now without formidable enemies anywhere. Our opponents on Mars and Venus having been

149

decisively defeated by our forces in the past two decades, we are now in a unique, historical position: the sole great power in the world of man. A period of unlimited peace and creative reconstruction seems inevitable."

He returned to the palace with the cheers of the Patronate ringing in his ears, his mood one of thoughtful jubilation. His spies had already reported that the patrons gave him a great deal of the credit for the victory on Venus. After all, the war had dragged on for a long time before his arrival. And then, abruptly, almost overnight, it had ended. The conclusion was that his brilliant leadership had made a decisive contribution. It required no astuteness for Tews to realize that, under such circumstances, he could generously bestow a triumph on Jerrin, and lose nothing by the other's honors.

Despite his own words to the Patronate, he found himself, as the peaceful weeks went by, progressively amazed at the reality of what he had said: No enemies. Nothing to fear. Even yet, it seemed hard to believe that the universe belonged to Linn; and that, as the Lord Adviser, he was now in his own sphere in a position of power over more subjects than any man had ever been. So it seemed to the dazzled Tews.

He would be a devoted leader, of course—he reassured himself hastily, disowning the momentary pride. He visualized great works that would reflect the glory of Linn and the golden age of Tews. The vision was so noble and inspiring, that for long he merely toyed with hazy, magnificent plans, and took no concrete action of any kind.

He was informed presently that Clane had returned from Venus. Shortly thereafter, he received a message from the mutation.

His Excellency,
Lord Adviser Tews
My most honored uncle:
    I should like to visit you and describe to you the result of several conversations between my brother, Jerrin, and

150

myself concerning potential dangers for the empire. They do not seem severe, but we are both concerned about the preponderance of slaves as against citizens on Earth, and we are unhappy about our lack of knowledge of the present situation among the peoples of the moons of Jupiter and Saturn.

Since these are the only dangers in sight, the sooner we examine every aspect of the problem the more certain we can be that the destiny of Linn will be under the control of intelligent action, and not governed in future by the necessary opportunism, which has been for so many generations the main element of government.

Your obedient nephew,
Clane

The letter irritated Tews. It seemed meddlesome. It reminded him that his control of Linn, and of the glorious future he envisaged for the empire, was not complete, and that in fact these nephews might urge compromises which would dim the beauty that only he, apparently, could see. Nevertheless, his reply was diplomatic:

My dear Clane:

It was a pleasure to hear from you, and as soon as I return from the mountains, I shall be happy to receive you and discuss all these matters in the most thoroughgoing fashion. I have instructed various departments to gather data, so that when we do get together, we can talk on the basis of facts.

Tews,
Lord Adviser

He actually issued the instructions, and actually listened to a brief account from an official who was an "expert" concerning conditions on the moons of Jupiter and Saturn. They were all inhabited by tribes in various stages of barbaric culture. Recent reports gleaned from questioning of primitives who came from there, and from the Linnan traders who visited certain ports of entry, indicated that the old game of intrigue and murder among tribal chieftans seeking ascendancy was still going on.

Relieved in spite of his previous conviction that the situation was exactly as it was now described, Tews departed on his mountain vacation with a retinue of three hundred courtiers and five hundred slaves. He was still there a month later, when a second message arrived from Clane.

Most gracious Lord Adviser Tews:

Your response to my message was a great relief to me. I wonder if I could further impose upon your good offices, and have your department heads determine how many visitors we have recently had from the moons, how many are still here, and where are they presently concentrated. The reason for this inquiry is that I have discovered that several of my agents on Europa, the great moon of Jupiter, were suddenly executed about a year ago, and that actually my own information from that territory is based upon reports, all of which are not less than two years old, and those are extremely vague. It seems that about five years ago, a new leader began to unify Europa; and my agents' reports—when I now examine the data they furnished—grew less clear with each month after that. I suspect that I have been victimized by carefully prepared propaganda. If this be so the fact that somebody was astute enough to seize my channels of information worries me.

These are only suspicions, of course, but it would seem advisable to have your people make inquiries with the possibility in mind that our present information sources are unreliable.

Your faithful servant, and nephew,
Clane

The reference to the mutation's "agents" reminded Tews unpleasantly that he lived in a world of spies. "I suppose," he thought wearily, "propaganda is even now being circulated against me, because I am on a vacation. People cannot possibly realize what great plans my engineers and I are making for the State on this so-called pleasure trip."

152

He wondered if, by releasing a series of public statements about the grandiose future, he might successfully head off criticism.

That irritation lasted for a day, and then he read Clane's letter again, and decided that an unruffled and diplomatic approach was desirable. He must ever be in a position to say that he invariably took the most thorough precaution against any eventuality.

He gave the necessary instructions, advised Clane that he had done so—and then began to consider seriously the situation that would exist when Jerrin returned from Venus six or eight months hence to receive his triumph. It no longer seemed quite the satisfactory prospect that it had been, when he himself had first returned from Venus. These nephews of his tended to interfere in State affairs, and indeed both had the legal right to be advisers of the government. Each, according to law, had a Council vote in Linnan affairs, although neither could directly interfere with administration.

"I suppose," Tews grudgingly acknowledged to himself, "Clane is within his rights; but what was it mother once said: 'It is an unwise man who always exercises his rights.'" He laughed, grimacing.

That night, just before he went to sleep, Tews had a flash of insight: "I'm slipping back into suspicion—the same fears that disturbed me when I was on Venus. I'm being influenced by this damnable palace atmosphere."

He felt personally incapable of base thoughts and accepted their presence in others—he told himself—with the greatest reluctance, and then only because of the possible effect on the State.

His sense of duty—that was the real pressure on him, he felt convinced. It compelled him to be aware of, and actually to look for, scheming and plotting, even though he was revolted by any indications of intrigue.

The realization of his own fundamental integrity reassured Tews. "After all," he thought, "I may occasionally be misled, but I cannot be wrong if I remain constantly on the alert for danger from all sources. And even a mutation with scientific knowledge and weapons is a matter about which I, as guardian of the State, must take cognizance."

He had already given considerable thought to the weapons he had seen Clane use on Venus. And during the days that followed, he came to the conclusion that he must take action. He kept saying to himself how reluctant he was to do so, but finally he advised Clane:

My dear nephew:

Although you have evidently not felt free to ask for the protection to which your rank, and the value of your work entitles you, I am sure you will be happy to hear that the State is prepared to undertake protection of the material which you have rescued from the pits of the gods, and from other ancient sources.

The safest place for all this material is at your residence in Linn. Accordingly, I am authorizing funds to transport to the city any such equipment which you have at your country estate. A guards unit will arrive at the estate within the week with adequate transport, and another guards unit is this day taking up guard duty at your town residence.

The captain of the guard, while of course responsible to me, will naturally grant you every facility for carrying on your work.

It is with pleasure, my dear Clane, that I extend to you this costly but earned protection.

At some time not too far in the future, I should like to have the privilege of a personally conducted tour, so that I may see for myself what treasures you have in your collection, with a view to finding further uses for them for the general welfare.

With cordial best wishes
Tews,
Lord Adviser

"At least," thought Tews, after he had dispatched the message, and given the necessary orders to the military forces, "that will for the present get the material all in one place.

Later, a further more stringent control is always possible—
not that it will ever be necessary, of course."

The wise leader simply planned for any contingency.
Even the actions of his most dearly beloved relatives must
be examined objectively.

He learned presently that Clane had offered no resistance,
and that the material had been transported to Linn without
incident.

He was still at the mountain palace of the Linns when a
third letter arrived from Clane. Though briefly stated, it
was a major social document. The preamble read:

To our uncle, the Lord Adviser:
It being the considered opinion of Lords Jerrin and
Clane Linn that a dangerous preponderance of slaves
exists in Linn, and that indeed the condition of slavery is
wholly undesirable in a healthy State, it is herewith pro-
posed that Lord Adviser Tews during his government lay
down as a guiding rule for future generations the following
principles:
1. All law-abiding human beings are entitled to the free
control of their own persons.
2. Where free control does not now obtain, it shall be
delivered to the individual on a rising scale, the first two
steps of which shall become effective immediately.
3. The first step shall be that no slave shall in future
be physically punished except by the order of a court.
4. The second step shall be that the slave's work day
shall not in future exceed ten hours a day.

The other steps outlined a method of gradually freeing the
slaves, until after twenty years only incorrigibles would be
"not free", and all of these would be controlled by the State
itself, under laws whereby each was dealt with "as an
individual."

Tews read the document with amazement and amusement.
He recalled another saying of his mother's: "Don't ever
worry about the idealists. The mob will cut their throats at
the proper moment."

His amusement faded rapidly. "These boys are really interfering in the affairs of state in Linn, itself, which is only remotely in their province." As, the summer over, he made preparations to return to the city, Tews scowlingly considered the threat "to the State," which—it seemed to him—was building up with alarming speed.

On the second day after his return to Linn, he received another letter from Clane. This one requested an audience to discuss "those matters relating to the defense of the empire, about which your departments have been gathering information."

What infuriated Tews about the letter was that the mutation was not even giving him time to settle down after his return. True, the work of re-establishment did not involve him—but it was a matter of courtesy to the office he held. On that level, Tews decided in an icy rage, Clane's persistence bore all the earmarks of a deliberate insult.

He sent a curt note in reply, which stated simply:

My dear Clane:

I will advise you as soon as I am free of the more pressing problems of administration. Please wait word from me.

Tews

He slept that night, confident that he was at last taking a firm stand, and that it was about time.

He awoke to news of disaster.

The only warning was a steely glinting of metal in the early morning sky. The invaders swooped down on the city of Linn in three hundred spaceships. There must have been advance spying, for they landed in force at the gates that were heavily guarded and at the main troop barracks inside the city. From each ship debouched two hundred odd men.

"Sixty thousand soldiers!" said Lord Adviser Tews after he had studied the reports. He issued instructions for the defense of the palace, and sent a carrier pigeon to the three legions encamped outside the city ordering two of them to attack when ready. And then he sat pale but composed watching the spectacle from a window which overlooked the hazy vastness of Linn proper.

Everything was vague and unreal. Most of the invading ships had disappeared behind large buidings. A few lay in the open, but they looked dead. It was hard to grasp that vicious fighting was going on in their vicinity. At nine o'clock, a messenger arrived from the Lady Lydia:

Dear Son:

Have you any news? Who is attacking us? Is it a limited assault, or an invasion of the empire? Have you contacted Clane?

L.

The first prisoner was brought in while Tews was scowling over the unpalatable suggestion that he seek the advice of his relative. The mutation was the last person he wanted to see. The prisoner, a bearded giant, proudly confessed that he was from Europa, one of the moons of Jupiter, and that he feared neither man nor god. The man's size and obvious physical prowess startled Tews. But his naive outlook on life was cheering. Subsequent prisoners had similar physical and mental characteristics. And so, long before noon, Tews had a fairly clear picture of the situation.

This was a barbarian invasion from Europa. It was obviously for loot only. But, unless he acted swiftly, Linn would be divested in a few days of treasures garnered over the centuries. Bloodthirsty commands flowed from Tews' lips. Put all prisoners to the sword. Destroy their ships, their weapons, their clothing. Leave not one vestige of their presence to pollute the eternal city.

The morning ran its slow course. Tews considered making an inspection of the city escorted by the palace cavalry. He abandoned the plan when he realized it would be impossible for commanders to send him reports if he were on the move. For the same reason he could not transfer his headquarters to a less clearly marked building. Just before noon, the relieving report arrived that two of three camp legions were attacking in force at the main gates.

The news steadied him. He began to think in terms of broader, more basic information about what had happened. He remembered unhappily that his departments probably had the information which—spurred by Clane—he had asked for months ago. Hastily, he called in several experts, and sat somberly while each of the men in turn told what he had learned.

There was actually a great deal of data. Europa, the great moon of Jupiter, had been inhabited from legendary times by fiercely quarreling tribes. Its vast atmosphere was said to have been created artificially with the help of the atom gods by the scientists of the golden age. Like all the artificial atmospheres, it contained a high proportion of the gas, teneol, which admitted sunlight, but did not allow much heat to escape into space.

Starting about five years before, travelers had begun to bring out reports of a leader named Czinczar who was ruthlessly welding all the hating factions of the planet into one nation. For a while it was such a dangerous territory that traders landed only at specified ports of entry. The information they received was that Czinczar's attempt at unification had failed. Contact grew even more vague after that; and it was clear to the listening Tews that the new leader had actually succeeded in his conquests, and that any word to the contrary was propaganda. The cunning Czinczar had seized outgoing communication sources and confused them while he consolidated his position among the barbarous forces of the planet.

Czinczar. The name had a sinister rhythm to it, a ring of leashed violence, a harsh, metallic tintinnabulation. If such a man and his followers escaped with even a fraction of the portable wealth of Linn, the inhabited solar system would echo with the exploit. The government of Lord Adviser Tews might tumble like a house of cards.

Tews had been hesitating. There was a plan in his mind that would work better if carried out in the dead of night. But that meant giving the attackers precious extra hours for loot. He decided not to wait, but dispatched a command to the third—still unengaged—camp legion to enter the tunnel that led into the central palace.

As a precaution, and with the hope of distracting the enemy leader, he sent a message to Czinczar in the care of a captured barbarian officer. In it he pointed out the foolishness of an attack that could only result in bloody reprisals on Europa itself, and suggested that there was still time for an honorable withdrawal. There was only one thing wrong with all these schemings. Czinczar had concentrated a large force of his own for the purpose of capturing the Imperial party. And had held back in the hope that he would learn definitely whether or not the Lord Adviser was inside the palace. The released prisoner, who delivered Tews' message, established his presence inside.

The attack in force that followed captured the Central Palace and everyone in it, and surprised the legionnaries who were beginning to emerge from the secret passageway. Czinczar's men poured all the oil in the large palace tanks into the downward sloping passageway, and set it afire.

Thus died an entire legion of men.

That night a hundred reserve barbarian spaceships landed behind the Linnan soldiers besieging the gates. And in the morning, when the barbarians inside the city launched an attack, the two remaining legions were cut to pieces.

Of these events the Lord Adviser Tews knew nothing. His skull had been turned over the previous day to Czinczar's favorite goldsmith, to be plated with Linnan gold, and shaped into a goblet to celebrate the greatest victory of the century.

20

To Lord Clane Linn, going over his accounts on his country estate, the news of the fall of Linn came as a special shock. With unimportant exceptions, all his atomic material was in Linn. He dismissed the messenger, who had unwisely shouted the news as he entered the door of the accounting department. And then sat at his desk—and realized that he had better accept for the time being the figures of his slave bookkeepers on the condition of the estate.

As he glanced around the room after announcing the postponement, it seemed to him that at least one of the slaves showed visible relief. He did not delay, but called the man before him instantly. He had an inexorable system in dealing with slaves, a system inherited from his long dead mentor, Joquin, along with the estate itself.

Integrity, hard work, loyalty, and a positive attitude produced better conditions, shorter working hours, more freedom of action, after thirty the right to marry, after forty legal freedom. Laziness and other negative attitudes such as cheating were punished by a set pattern of demotions. Short of changing the law of the land, Clane could not at the moment imagine a better system, in view of the existence of slavery. And now, in spite of his personal anxieties, he carried out the precept of Joquin as it applied to a situation where no immediate evidence was available. He told the man, Oorag, what had aroused his suspicions, and asked him if they were justified. "If you are guilty and confess," he said, "you will receive only one demotion. If you do not confess and you are later proven guilty, there will be three demotions, which means physical labor, as you know."

The slave, a big man, shrugged, and said with a sneer, "By the time Czinczar is finished with you Linnans, you will be working for me."

"Field labor," said Clane curtly, "for three months, ten hours a day."

It was no time for mercy. An empire under attack did not flinch from the harshest acts. Anything that could be construed as weakness would be disastrous.

As the slave was led out by guards, he shouted a final insult over his shoulder. "You wretched mutation," he said, "you'll be where you belong when Czinczar gets here."

Clane did not answer. He considered it doubtful that the new conqueror had been selected by fate to punish all the evildoers of Linn according to their desserts. It would take too long. He put the thought out of his mind, and walked to the doorway. There he paused, and faced the dozen trusted slaves who sat at their various desks.

"Do nothing rash," he said slowly in a clear voice, "any of you. If you harbor emotions similar to those expressed by Oorag, restrain yourselves. The fall of one city in a surprise attack is not important." He hesitated. He was, he realized, appealing to their cautious instincts, but his reason told him that in a great crisis men did not always consider all the potentialities.

"I am aware," he said finally, "there is no great pleasure in being a slave, though it has advantages—economic security, free craft training. But Oorag's wild words are a proof that, if young slaves were free to do as they pleased, they would constitute a jarring, if not revolutionary factor in the community. It is unfortunately true that people of different races can only gradually learn to live together."

He went out, satisfied that he had done the best possible under the circumstances. He had no doubt whatsoever that here, in this defiance of Oorag, the whole problem of a slave empire had again shown itself in miniature. If Czinczar were to conquer any important portion of Earth, a slave uprising would follow automatically. There were too many slaves, far too many for safety, in the Linnan empire.

Outside, he saw his first refugees. They were coming down near the main granaries in a variety of colorful sky-scooters. Clane watched them for a moment, trying to picture their departure from Linn. The amazing thing was that they had waited till the forenoon of the second day. People must simply have refused to believe that the city was in danger, though, of course, early fugitives could have fled in other directions. And so not come near the estate.

Clane emerged decisively out of his reverie. He called a slave, and dispatched him to the scene of the arrivals with a command to his personal guards. "Tell these people who have rapid transportation to keep moving. Here, eighty miles from Linn we shall take care only of the foot-weary."

Briskly now, he went into his official residence, and called the commanding officer of his troops. "I want volunteers," he explained, "particularly men with strong religious beliefs, who on this second night after the invasion are prepared to fly into Linn and remove all the transportable equipment from my laboratory."

His plan, as he outlined it finally to some forty volunteers, was simplicity itself. In the confusion of taking over a vast city, it would probably be several days before the barbarian army would actually occupy all the important residences. Particularly, on these early days, they might miss a house situated, as his was, behind a barrier of trees.

If by some unfortunate chance it was already occupied, it would probably be so loosely held that bold men could easily kill every alien on the premises, and so accomplish their purpose.

"I want to impress upon you," Clane went on, "the importance of this task. As all of you know, I am a member of the temple hierarchy. I have been entrusted with sacred god metals and sacred equipment, including material taken from the very homes of the gods. It would be a disaster if these precious relics were to fall into unclean hands. I, therefore, charge you that, if you should by some mischance be captured, do not reveal the real purpose of your presence. Say that you came to rescue your owner's private property. Even admit you were foolish to sacrifice yourself for such a reason."

Mindful of Tews' guard unit, he finished his instructions: "It may be that Linnan soldiers are guarding the equipment, in which case give the officer in command this letter."

He handed the document to the captain of the volunteers. It was an authorization signed by Clane with the seal of his rank. Since the death of Tews, such an authorization would not be lightly ignored.

When they had gone out to prepare for the mission, Clane dispatched one of his private spaceships to the nearby city of Goram, and asked the commander there, a friend of his, what kind of counter-action was being prepared against the invader. "Are the authorities in the cities and towns," he asked, "showing that they understand the patterns of action required of them in a major emergency? Or must the old law be explained to them from the beginning?"

The answer arrived in the shortest possible time, something under forty minutes. The general placed his forces at Clane's command, and advised that he had dispatched messengers to every major city on Earth, in the name of "his excellency, Lord Clane Linn, ranking survivor on Earth of the noble Tews, the late Lord Adviser, who perished at the head of his troops, defending the city of Linn from the foul and murderous surprise attack launched by a barbarian horde of beast-like men, who seek to destroy the fairest civilization that ever existed."

There was more in the same vein, but it was not the excess of verbiage that startled Clane. It was the offer itself, and the implications. *In his name,* an army was being organized.

After rereading the the message, he walked slowly to the full length mirror in the adjoining bathroom, and stared at his image. He was dressed in the fairly presentable reading gown of a temple scientist. Like all his temple clothing, the shoulder cloth folds of this concealed his "differences" from casual view. An observer would have to be very acute to see how carefully the cloak was drawn around his neck, and how it was built up to hide the slant of his body from the neck down, and how tightly the arm ends were tied together at his wrists.

It would take three months to advise Lord Jerrin on Venus, and four to reach Lord Draid on Mars, both planets being on the far side of the sun from Earth. It would require almost, but not quite, twice as long to receive a message from them. Only a member of the ruling family could possibly win the support of the diversified elements of the empire. Of the fate of the Lord Adviser's immediate family, there was as yet no word. Besides, they were women. Which left Lord Clane, youngest brother of Jerrin, grandson of the late Lord Leader. For not less than six months accordingly he would be the acting Lord Leader of Linn.

The afternoon of that second day of the invasion waned slowly. Great ships began to arrive, bringing soldiers. By dusk, more than a thousand men were encamped along the road to the city of Linn, and by the riverside. Darting small craft and wary full-sized spaceships floated overhead, and foot patrols were out, guarding all approaches to the estate.

The roads themselves were virtually deserted. It was too soon for the mobs from Linn, which air-scooter scouts reported were fleeing the captured city by the gates that, at mid-afternoon, were still open.

During the last hour before dark, the air patrols reported that the gates were being shut one by one. And that the stream of refugees was dwindling to a trickle near the darkening city. All through that last hour, the sky was free of scooters transporting refugees. It seemed clear that the people who could afford the costly machines were either already safe, or had waited too long, possibly in the hope of succoring some absent member of the family.

At midnight, the volunteers departed on their dangerous mission in ten scooters and one spaceship. As a first gesture of his new authority, Clane augmented their forces by adding a hundred soldiers from the regular army. He watched the shadowy ships depart, then hurried to attend a meeting of those general officers who had had time to arrive. A dozen men climbed to their feet as he entered. They saluted, then stood at attention.

Clane stopped short. He had intended to be calm, matter-of-fact; pretending even to himself that what was happening was natural. The feeling wasn't like that. An emotion came, familiar, terrifying. He could feel it tingling up the remoter reflexes of his nervous system as of old, the beginning of the dangerous childish panic, product of his early, horrible days as a tormented mutation. The muscles of his face worked. Three times he swallowed with difficulty. Then, with a stiff gesture, he returned the salute. And, walking hastily to the head of the table, sat down.

Clane waited till they had seated themselves, then asked for brief reports as to available troops. He noted down the figures given by each man for his province, and at the end added up the columns.

"With four provinces still to be heard from," he announced, "we have a total of eighteen thousand trained soldiers, six thousand partly trained reserves, and some five hundred thousand able-bodied civilians."

"Your excellency," said his friend, Morkid, "the Linnan empire maintains normally a standing army of one million men. On Earth by far the greatest forces were stationed in or near the city of Linn, and they have been annihilated. Some four hundred thousand men are still on Venus, and slightly more than two hundred thousand on Mars."

Clane, who had been mentally adding up the figures given, said quickly: "That doesn't add up to a million men."

Morkid nodded gravely. "For the first time in years, the army is under strength. The conquest of Venus seemed to eliminate all potential enemies of Linn, and Lord Adviser Tews considered it a good time to economize."

"I see," said Clane. He felt pale and bloodless, like a man who has suddenly discovered that he cannot walk by himself.

165

21

Lydia climbed heavily out of her sedan chair, conscious of how old and unattractive she must seem to the grinning barbarians in the courtyard. She didn't let it worry her too much. She had been old a long time now, and her image in a mirror no longer shocked her. The important thing was that her request for an interview had been granted by Czinczar after she had, at his insistence, withdrawn the proviso that she be given a safe conduct.

The old woman smiled mirthlessly. She no longer valued highly the combination of skin and bones that was her body. But there was exhilaration in the realization that she was probably going to her death. Despite her age, and some self-disgust, she felt reluctant to accept oblivion. But Clane had asked her to take the risk. It vaguely amazed Lydia that the idea of the mutation holding the Lord Leadership did not dismay her any more. She had her own private reasons for believing Clane capable. She walked slowly along the familiar hallways, through the gleaming arches and across rooms that glittered with the treasures of the Linn family. Everywhere were the big, bearded young men who had come from far Europa to conquer an empire about which they could only have heard by hearsay. Looking at them, she felt justified in all the pitiless actions she had taken in her day. They were, it seemed to the grim old woman, living personifications of the chaos that she had fought against all her life.

As she entered the throne room, the darker thoughts faded from her mind. She glanced around with sharp eyes for the mysterious leader. There was no one on or near the throne. Groups of men stood around talking. In one of the groups was a tall, graceful, young man, different from all the others in the room. They were bearded. He was clean shaven.

He saw her, and stopped listening to what one of his companions was saying, stopped so noticeably that a silence fell on the group. The silence communicated itself to other groups. After not more than a minute, the roomful of men had faced about and was staring at her, waiting for their commander to speak. Lydia waited also, examining him swiftly. Czinczar was not a handsome man, but he had an appearance of strength, always a form of good looks. And yet it was not enough. This barbarian world was full of strong-looking men. Lydia, who had expected outstanding qualities, was puzzled.

His face was sensitive rather than brutal, which was unusual. But still not enough to account for the fact that he was absolute lord of an enormous undisciplined horde.

The great man came forward. "Lady," he said, "you have asked to see me."

And then she knew his power. In all her long life, she had never heard a baritone voice so resonant, so wonderfully beautiful, so assured of command. It changed him. She realized suddenly that she had been mistaken about his looks. She had sought normal clean-cut handsomeness. This man was beautiful.

The first fear came to her. A voice like that, a personality like that—

She had a vision of this man persuading the Linnan empire to do his will. Mobs hypnotized. The greatest men bewitched. She broke the spell with an effort of will. She said, "You are Czinczar?"

"I am Czinczar."

The definite identification gave Lydia another though briefer pause. But this time she recovered more swiftly. And this time, also, her recovery was complete. Her eyes narrowed. She stared at the great man with a developing hostility. "I can see," she said acridly, "that my purpose in coming to see you is going to fail."

"Naturally." Czinczar inclined his head, shrugged. He did not ask her what was her purpose. He seemed incurious. He stood politely, waiting for her to finish what she had to say.

"Until I saw you," said Lydia grimly, "I took it for granted that you were an astute general. Now, I see that you consider yourself a man of destiny. I can already see you being lowered into your grave."

There was an angry murmur from the other men in the room. Czinczar waved them into silence. "Madam," he said, "such remarks are offensive to my officers. State your case, and then I will decide what to do with you."

Lydia nodded, but she noted that he did not say that he was offended. She sighed inwardly. She had her mental picture now of this man, and it depressed her. All through known history these natural leaders had been spewed up by the inarticulate masses. They had a will in them to rule or die. But the fact that they frequently died young made no great difference. Their impact on their times was colossal. Such a man could, even in his death throes, drag down long established dynasties with him. Already, he had killed the legal ruler of Linn, and struck a staggering blow at the heart of the empire. By a military freak, it was true—but history accepted such accidents without a qualm.

Lydia said quietly, "I shall be brief, since you are no doubt planning high policy and further military campaigns. I have come here at the request of my grandson, Lord Clane Linn."

"The mutation!" Czinczar nodded. His remark was noncommittal, an identification, not a comment.

Lydia felt an inward shock that Czinczar's knowledge of the ruling faction should extend to Clane, who had tried to keep himself in the background of Linnan life. She dared not pause to consider the potentialities. She continued quietly, "Lord Clane is a temple scientist, and, as such, he has for many years been engaged in humanitarian scientific experiments. Most of his equipment, unfortunately, is here in Linn." Lydia shrugged. "It is quite valueless to you and your men, but it would be a great loss to civilization if it were destroyed or casually removed. Lord Clane therefore requests that you permit him to send slaves to his town house to remove these scientific instruments to his country estate. In return—"

"Yes," echoed Czinczar, "in return—"

His tone was ever so faintly derisive; and Lydia had a sudden realization that he was playing with her. It was not a possibility that she could pay any attention to.

"In return," she said, "he will pay you in precious metals and jewels any reasonable price which you care to name." Having finished, she took a deep breath, and waited.

There was a thoughtful expression on the barbarian leader's face. "I have heard," he said, "of Lord Clane's experiments with the so-called"—he hesitated—"god metals of Linn. Very curious stories, some of them; and as soon as I am free from my military duties I intend to examine this laboratory with my own eyes. You may tell your grandson," he continued with a tone of finality, "that his little scheme to retrieve the greatest treasures in the entire Linnan empire was hopeless from the beginning. Five spaceships descended in the first few minutes of the attack on the estate of Lord Clane, to insure that the mysterious weapons there were not used against my invading fleet, and I consider it a great misfortune that he himself was absent in the country at the time. You may tell him that we were not caught by surprise by his midnight attempt two days ago to remove the equipment, and that his worst fears as to its fate are justified." He finished, "It is a great relief to know that most of his equipment is safely in our hands."

Lydia said nothing. The phrase, "You may tell him," had had a profound chemical effect on her body.

She hadn't realized she was so tense. It seemed to her that, if she spoke, she would reveal her own tremendous personal relief. *"You may tell him—"* There could be only one interpretation. She was going to be allowed to depart. Once more she waited.

Czinczar walked forward until he was standing directly in front of her. Something of his barbarous origin, so carefully suppressed until now, came into his manner. A hint of a sneer, the contempt of a physically strong man for decadence, a feeling of genuine basic superiority to the refinement that was in Lydia. When he spoke, he showed that he was consciously aware that he was granting mercy.

"Old woman," he said, "I am letting you go because you did me a great favor when you maneuvered your son, Lord Tews, into the—what did he call it—Lord Advisership. That move, and that alone, gave me the chance I needed to make my attack on the vast Linnan empire." He smiled. "You may depart, bearing that thought in mind."

For some time, Lydia had condemned the sentimental action that had brought Tews into supreme power. But it was a different matter to realize that, far away in interplanetary space, a man had analyzed the move as a major Linnan disaster. She went out without another word.

Czinczar slowly climbed the hill leading up to the low, ugly fence that fronted Lord Clane's town house. He paused at the fence, recognized the temple building material of which it was composed—and then walked on thoughtfully. With the same narrow-eyed interest a few minutes later, he stared at the gushing fountain of boiling water. He beckoned finally the engineer who had directed the construction of the spaceships that had brought his army to Earth. "How does it work?" he asked.

The designer examined the base of the fountain. He was in no hurry, a big fattish man with a reputation for telling jokes so coarse that strong men winced with shame. He had already set up house in one of the great palaces with three Linnan girls as mistresses and a hundred Linnan men and women as slaves. He was a happy man, with little personal conceit and very little pride as yet to restrain his movements. He located the opening into the fountain, and knelt in the

170

dirt like any worker. In that, however, he was not unique. Czinczar knelt beside him, little realizing how his actions shocked the high-born Linnans who belonged to his personal slave retinue. The two men peered into the gloom. "Temple building material," said Meewan, the designer.

Czinczar nodded. They climbed to their feet without further comment, for these were matters which they had discussed at length over a period of years. At the house, a few minutes later, the leader and his henchman both lifted the heavy draperies that covered the walls of a corridor leading into the main laboratory. Like the fence outside, the walls were warm as from some inner heat.

Temple building material! Once again no comment passed between them. They walked on into the laboratory proper; and now they looked at each other in amazement. The room had been noticeably enlarged from its original size, although this they did not know. A great section had been torn out of one wall, and the gap, although it was completely filled in, was still rough and unfinished. But that was only the environment. On almost every square yard of the vast new floor were machines opaque and machines transparent, machines big and small, some apparently complete, other unmistakably mere fragments.

For a moment there was a distinct sense of too much to see. Czinczar walked forward speculatively, glanced at several of the transparent articles with an eye that tried to skim the essentials of shape and inner design. At no time, during those first moments, did he have any intention of pausing for a detailed examination. And then, out of the corner of his eye, he caught a movement.

A glow. He bent down, and peered into a long partly transparent metal case, roughly shaped like a coffin, even as to the colorful and costly looking lining. The inside, however, curved down to form a narrow channel. Along this channel rolled a ball of light. It turned over sedately, taking approximately one minute to cover the distance to the far side. With the same lack of haste, it paused, seemed to meditate on its

171

next action, and then, with immense deliberation began its return journey.

The very meaninglessness of the movement fascinated Czinczar. He extended his hand gingerly to within an inch of the ball. Nothing happened. He drew back, and pursed his lips. In spite of his attack on Linn, he was not a man who took risks. He beckoned towards a guard. "Bring a slave," he said. Under his direction a former Linnan nobleman, perspiring from every pore, extended his finger and touched the moving ball. His finger went in as if there were nothing there.

He drew back, startled. But the inexorable Czinczar was not through with him. Once more the reluctant, though no longer quite so fearful, finger penetrated the moving ball. The ball rolled into it, through it, beyond it. Czinczar motioned the slave aside, and stood looking at him thoughtfully. There must have been something of his purpose in his face, for the man gave a low cry of horror: "Master, I understand nothing of what I have seen. Nothing. Nothing."

"Kill him," said Czinczar.

He turned, scowling, back to the machine. "There must be," he said, and there was a stubborn note in his glorious voice, "some reason for its movements, for—its existence."

Half an hour later, he was still examining it.

22

"If I could only—" thought Clane many times. And knew that he dared not. Not yet.

He had with a certain cynicism permitted the soldiers sent by Lord Tews to remove his equipment to Linn. This included the prize of all his findings, a ball that rolled to and fro in a coffin-like container; a discovery of the golden age which had shaken his certainties to the core of his being.

Because of the ball of energy, he had not hesitated to let Tews take control of the artifacts of that ancient and wonderful culture.

He need merely go into the presence of the ball, and because of his knowledge of its function, could attune himself to it.

It could then be mentally controlled from a distance; all its strange power available—for about three days. At some not precisely determinable time on the third day, it would cease to "come" when he "called" it.

Then he would have to visit it while it was in its container, and by direct contact re-establish rapport.

It had seemed evident from Tews' action that the Lord Adviser had not intended to bar him from the equipment. And so, the location of the ball in his own Linnan residence under guard had not mattered.

He had not despite his anxieties anticipated a major attack that would capture Linn in one swift assault.

And so, the weapon that could end the war was out of his reach, unless he could somehow get to it by cunning means.

He did not yet feel that desperate.

Nor actually were the Linnan forces strong enough to take advantage of a miracle.

Even as in a kind of mental agony, he wondered how he would get into Linn, and into his house, he devoted himself to the grim business of training an army as it fought.

There was an old saying in the Linnan army to the effect that, during his first month, a trainee, if put into battle, caused the death of his trained companions. During the second month, he hindered retreats made necessary by his presence. And during the third month he was just good enough to get himself killed in the first engagement.

Clane, watching a group of trainees after several weeks of drilling, experienced all the agony of realizing how true the adage was. Learning to fire a bow effectively required complex integration of mind and body. In-fighting with swords had to include the capacity for co-operating with companions. And effective spear fighting was an art in itself.

The plan he outlined that night to the full general staff was an attempt to cover up against the weakness. It was a frank determination to use unfit men as first-line defense troops. He put in a word for the unfit. "Do not over-exercise them. Get them out into the open air, and simply teach them the first elements of how to use weapons. First, bows and arrows, then spears, and finally swords."

After the meeting, long into the night, he examined reports on the cities of Nouris and Gulf, which had fallen virtually without a fight. As the barbarians attacked, the slaves simply rose up and murdered their masters. A supplementary general staff report recommended mass execution for all able-bodied male slaves.

The uneasy Clane dispatched messengers to gather commercial and industrial leaders for a morning conference, and then unhappily took the slave problem to bed with him.

At 10 o'clock he called the meeting to order, and told the hundred-odd assembled representative merchants that the army had recommended universal death for male slaves.

His statement caused an immediate uproar.

One man said: "Your excellency, it is impossible. We cannot destroy so much valuable property."

With two exceptions, that seemed to be the attitude. Both exceptions were young men, one of whom said: "Gentlemen, this is a necessary action."

The other said: "My own feeling is that this crisis makes possible a great progressive act—the end of slavery in Linn."

Both men were shouted down by enraged merchants.

Clane stepped forward, and raised his hand. When he had silence, he began: "There is no time for half measures. We must adopt one or the other of these alternatives."

There followed a series of conferences among groups of merchants. Finally, a bland spokesman said: "Your excellency, the merchants here present favor *promising* the slaves freedom."

For a long moment, Clane gazed at his grinning audience,

174

then abruptly turned his back on them, and left the room. That afternoon he prepared a special bulletin:

FREEDOM FOR LOYAL
SERVANTS

By order of his excellency, Lord Clane Linn, Leader of Linn, temple scientist, beloved of the Atom Gods themselves, it is hereby commanded, and so it shall be forevermore:

GREETINGS to all those good men and women who have quietly and efficiently served the empire in atonement for sins of leaders who rashly led them into hopeless wars against the god-protected Linnan empire—here is the chance for complete freedom which you have earned by your actions and attitudes during the past years.

The empire has been attacked by a cruel and barbarous invader. His reign of terror cannot but be temporary, for invincible forces are gathering against him. An army of a million men is on the way from Mars and Venus, and here on Earth irresistible forces totaling more than two million men are already organizing for battle.

The enemy numbers less than sixty thousand soldiers. To this small army, which gained its initial victory by a surprise and base attack, a few foolish men and women have rashly attached themselves. All the women unless they are convicted of major crimes, will be spared. For the men who have already gone over to the enemy, there is but one hope: Escape immediately from the barbarian enemy, and REPORT TO THE CONCENTRATION CAMPS listed at the bottom of this proclamation. There will be no guards at the camps, but weekly roll calls will be made. And every man whose name appears regularly on these rolls will be granted full freedom when the enemy is defeated.

For hardened recalcitrants, the penalty is death.

To those men and women still loyally serving at their appointed tasks, I, Lord Clane, acting Lord Leader of Linn, give the following commands:

175

All women and children will remain at their present residences, continuing to serve as in the past.

All men report to their masters, and say, "It is my intention to take advantage of the offer of Lord Clane. Give me a week's food, so that I, too, may report to a concentration camp."

Having done this, and having received the food, leave at once. DO NOT DELAY A SINGLE HOUR.

If for some reason your master is not at home, take the food and go without permission. No one will hinder you in your departure from the city.

Any man to whom this order applies, who is found lurking within any city or town twenty-four hours after this proclamation is posted, will be suspected of treasonable intent.

The penalty is death.

Any man, who after one week, is found within a fifty mile radius of a city, will be suspected of treasonable intent.

The penalty is death.

To save yourself, go to a concentration camp, and appear regularly for roll call. If the barbarians attack your camp, scatter into the forests and hills and hide, or go to another camp. Adequate food rations will be supplied all camps.

All those of proven loyalty will receive freedom when the war is over. They will immediately have the right to marry. Settlement land will be opened up. After five years, citizenship rights, granted alien immigrants, will be available on application.

This is the end of slavery in the Linnan empire.

BE WISE—BE SAFE—BE FREE

It was a document that had its weak points. Before issuing it, Clane spent time arguing its merits to a group of doubtful officers—he ignored the merchants; they were too venal to be considered. He pointed out that it would be impossible to keep secret a general order for mass execution. A majority of the slaves would escape, and then they would really be dangerous. He admitted that the proclamation, though he meant every word of the promise in it, was full of lies. A million slaves in Linn alone had gone over to Czinczar, many of them trained soldiers. Czinczar could use them to garrison any city he might capture, and thus have his own army free for battle. It was Morkid, sardonic and scathing, who ended the argument late in the afternoon.

"Gentlemen," he said, "you do not seem to be aware that our commander-in-chief has at one stroke cut through all our illusions and false hopes, and penetrated straight to the roots of the situation in which we find ourselves. What is clear by the very nature of our discussion is that we have no choice." His voice went up: "In this period when disaster is so imminent, we are fortunate in having as our leader a genius of the first rank, who has already set us on the only military path that can lead to victory.

"Gentlemen"—his voice rang with the tribute—"I give you Lord Clane Linn, acting Lord Leader of Linn."

The clapping lasted for five minutes.

23

Clane watched the battle for Goram from a patrol craft that darted from strong point to strong point. Enemy squadrons tried again and again to close in on him, but his own machine was faster and more maneuverable.

The familiar trick of getting above him was tried, an old device in patrol craft and spaceship fighting. But the expected energy flow upward did not take place. His small vessel did not even sag, which was normally the minimum reaction when two sources of atomic energy operated on a gravity line.

The efforts worried Clane. Czinczar was, of course, aware by this time that his enemy knew more about the metals of the gods than he or his technicians. But it would be unfortunate if they should conclude from the actions of this one ship that Clane himself was inside. He wanted to see this battle. In spite of everything, minute by minute, he saw it.

The defense was tough, tougher than he had anticipated from the fact that four more cities had fallen in the past four weeks. The untrained were fighting grimly for their lives. Arrows took a toll of the attackers. Spears, awkwardly but desperately manipulated, inflicted wounds and sometimes death. The sword fighting stage was the worst. The muscular and powerful barbarians, once they penetrated the weapons that could attack them from a distance, made short work of their weaker adversaries.

The first line was down, devastated, defeated. The second line battle began. Barbarian reserves came forward, and were met by waves of arrows that darkened the sky—and took their toll when they struck the advancing groups of men. Hoarse cries of pain, curses, the shrieks of the desperately wounded, the agonized horror of Linnans suddenly cut off, and doomed, rose up to the ears of those in the darting small craft. The defenders strove to stay together. That was part of their instructions. Retreat slowly to the central squares—which were strongly held against a surprise rear attack.

Retreat, and at the last minute spaceships would land and rescue the hard-pressed, but theoretically still intact army of what had once been able-bodied civilians. After a month and a half of training, they were too valuable to sacrifice in a last ditch fight.

As it was, their dogged resistance was shaping the pattern of the war. Surely, Czinczar, counting his men after each battle, must already be having his own private doubts. His army as a whole, augmented by the unrepentant among the slaves, was increasing daily. But the larger the army grew the smaller was his chance of controlling it.

Yet there was no doubt about this battle, or this city. As the dark tide of night slipped in from the east, victory fires began to burn in all the important streets. The smoke wreathed into the sky and blood-red flames licked up into the blackness. The Linnans below, at this very moment enduring the beginning of a barbarian occupation, would not be in a humor to appreciate that their grudgingly accepted defeat represented a possible turning point in the war.

The time had come to decide when and where and under what conditions the main Linnan force would be thrown into a decisive battle for the control of the planet. And there was another decision, also, involving an immensely risky attempt to get near the ball of light. Clane shifted uneasily and drew his cloak tightly around his thin shoulders.

He was still considering ways and means when a message was brought him by a released Linnan nobleman, who had been captured by the barbarians.

The message was a one-sentence question from Czinczar: "Have you ever wondered, my dear Lord Clane, how the civilization of the golden age was so *completely* destroyed?"

It was a problem about which Clane had pondered many times. But it had never occured to him that the answer might be known to a barbarian from a remote moon of Jupiter.

He questioned the released nobleman, a middle-aged knight of the empire, as to conditions in Linn. The answers were not pleasant. Many slaves had taken revenge on their former masters. Numerous Linnan women of rank had been reduced to the status of prostitute.

In questioning the man for any news of his Linnan residence, he learned that Czinczar had publicly invited temple scientists to take care of "certain relics" formerly in the possession of Lord Clane.

Clane said at that point: "He actually mentioned my name."

"It was posted," was the reply, and the man shrugged. "I read it, on one of my errands out of the palace grounds."

Long after the interview was over, Clane considered that. He suspected a trap—and yet, Czinczar could not know how immensely valuable that sphere was.

If the barbarian leader had looked into it through a hollow tube, he might be startled at what was "inside". But still it would do him no good.

Nevertheless, suppose it was a trap.

It still made no difference. For his purpose, momentary proximity to the ball was all that would be required. Dared he take the chance?

He was still considering the gamble when another released nobleman brought a second message from Czinczar:

"I shall like to have a conversation with you, and should like to show you an object the like of which—I'll wager—you have never seen. Can you think of a way in which such a meeting could be arranged?"

Lord Clane showed the message to the general staff at its meeting the following morning. They unanimously forbade such a rendezvous, but agreed that it was an opportunity to send a formal message to the barbarian leader.

The mutation, who had his own reasons for appearing firm, had already written the communication. He read it to the assembled officers:

To the barbarian chieftain, Czinczar:

Your cowardly attempt to win mercy for your crimes against humanity by a personal appeal to myself, is of no avail. Get off this planet with your barbarous forces. Only immediate compliance can save you and Europa from destruction. Take heed!

Clane,
Acting Lord Leader

The message was approved, and dispatched in the care of a captured barbarian officer. Clane began immediately to complete preparations for launching an attack against the city of Linn. Such an attack had been discussed several times by the staff; and had been agreed on reluctantly, as

180

a feint. The generals felt that a landing might confuse the defenders of the city, and thus enable the Linnan army to recapture key outlying cities; which would indeed be the real goal. It was understood that the assault force would withdraw from Linn during the night of the day of attack.

Clane was content with this. He set out for the city of Linn the day before the attack, making the initial part of the journey in an air scooter. From this, in a secluded spot, he unloaded a donkey and a cart of vegetables, and trudged beside it the final twelve miles.

In his drab work garb of a temple initiate, his was one of many carts; and at no time was there any problem. So vast was the slave army that held Linn, that Czinczar's forces had quickly sought to establish a normal flow of food from the surrounding countryside into the city to ward off starvation.

Linnan scouts had long since reported that the gates were open.

Clane entered without interference from the former slaves who guarded that particular gate. Once inside, he was even less conspicuous, and no one questioned his right to go along the street towards his city residence. He climbed the hill at the trades entrance, and was permitted to take his cart through an opening in the low fence by the single barbarian soldier who guarded that section of it.

Dutifully, as if he were sent on lawful business, he headed for the trades entrance of the house, and he turned the vegetables over to two women, and said, "Who is in charge today?"

He was given a barbarian name: "Gleedon!"

"Where is he?" Clane asked.

"In the office, of course—through there." The older woman pointed along the main hallway, which led through the large central room where most of the precious machinery and equipment had been stored.

As he entered the great room, he saw that there were a dozen barbarian soldiers at the various entrances. He saw also that the container with the ball of light was at the center of the chamber.

...Misty sphere, vaguely glowing as if from an inner flame, rolling to and fro...

He could walk by, and touch it, in passing.

Without appearing too hurried, he walked forward, put his finger through the flimsy surface of the sphere, and, without pausing, continued on toward the office.

He was sorely tempted, at this point, to take no further chances. If he acted at once, and seized the house, then he would have control of the box.

But if he carried through with his original plan, and then the box were removed, so that he could not find it during the three days that the sphere would now be activated—He shuddered, and refused to think of such an eventuality.

He had been impressed by Czinczar's communications. The barbarian leader had important information to give. Somehow, somewhere, he had gotten hold of an object so valuable that he had risked his self-esteem in attempting to establish contact.

If too hasty action were taken, that knowledge might be lost.

Even as he walked on through the room, the mutation silently reaffirmed his purpose. A moment later, he entered the office, and informed the barbarian officer there, that he had come for the job of taking care of the relics of the atom gods.

The big man stood up, and squinted down at him, gave an almost naive start of recognition, and then called two soldiers from the hallway.

And then he said: "Lord Clane Linn, you are under arrest."

To one of the soldiers he commanded: "Get ropes. Tie him up."

Meekly, the mutation submitted to being bound.

24

The moment the news arrived, Czinczar headed for Linn. He was met on the roof of the central palace by Meewan. The big man had a smile on his plump, good-fellow face. "Your theory was right," he said admiringly. "You thought he would take a chance at the critical period of the invasion. He arrived this morning."

"Tell me exactly how you accepted his services." The golden voice spoke softly. The strange face was thoughtful as the other man gave his detailed account. There seemed no end to his interest. When the story was finished, he asked question after question. Each answer seemed merely to stimulate new questions. Meewan said finally, querulously:

"Your excellency, I have no doubt that our men have put the best face on the capture, to make themselves look good. They claim to have captured him as he entered the building, before he could do anything, or touch anything. Since they're a lax bunch of rascals, I question this. But what does it matter? What are you doubtful about?"

That gave Czinczar pause; he had not realized how tense he was. After all, he told himself, the situation was simple enough. He had issued an open invitation for temple scientists to come and take care of "some god-metal relics" which had fallen into possession of the conquerors. It was a cleverly worded request, designed to win general approval from the defeated even as it drew *the* temple scientist to his own undoing. Its only stipulation, very guardedly worded, was that in return for the privilege of sharing the "safeguarding of the relics," experiments should be continued as if no war were being waged.

"The gods," Czinczar had said sanctimoniously in the invitation, "are above the petty quarrels of mankind."

Apparently, at least one of its purposes was accomplished. The mutation himself had applied for the job. Czinczar meditated cautiously on tactics. "Bring him here," he said finally. "We can't take any risks of his having established control over anything at his house. We know too little and he too much."

While he waited, he examined the rod of force—which was one of the few workable instruments that had been found in the house. He was not a man who accepted past truths as final. The fact that it had worked a week ago did not mean that it would work now. He tested it from a great window, pointing it at the upper foliage of a nearby tree. No sound, no visible light spewed forth—but the upper section of the tree crashed down onto a pathway below. Czinczar experienced the satisfaction of a logical man whose logic had proved correct. It was not an uncommon satisfaction. From the early days when he had been a back country transcriber of messages to the days of his rise to power, he had taken risks which seemed necessary, no more, no less. Even now he could not be sure that the atomic wizard, Lord Clane, would not defeat him by some decisive wile. For several minutes, he pondered that, and then ordered a box brought in from the ice room of the palace. The contents of the box had come all the way from Europa packed in ice. He was indicating to the slaves where to place the box when an officer burst breathlessly into the throne room.

"Excellency," he cried. "Hundreds of spaceships. It's an attack."

Standing at the window a moment later, watching the ships settling down, Czinczar realized that his hazy suspicions had been correct. The appearance of Clane in the city was part of a planned maneuver, which would now run its deadly course. It was a pleasure to know that Lord Clane himself was caught in a trap.

He wasted no time watching a battle which he could not hope to see from the palace in any important detail. Nor did he have the feeling Tews had had months earlier, that it was necesary for commanders to know where he was in the early stages of the engagement. He issued quick instructions ordering the ice-packed box sent after him, and wrote a note for Meewan. Then he rode with a strong escort to the headquarters of the reserve army in the middle of the city.

The reserve contained a barbarian core, but, like the main defense of the city, it was overwhelmingly made up of slaves. Czinczar's arrival was greeted by a roar of excitement. The cheers did not die down until long after he had entered the building.

He talked over the situation with some of the slave officers, and found them calm and confident. According to their estimates sixty thousand Linnan soldiers had landed in the first wave. The fact that that was exactly the number of barbarians who had originally invaded the city did not seem to occur to the slaves. But the comparison struck Czinczar sharply. He wondered if it was designed to have some symbolical meaning. The possibility made him sardonic. Not symbols but swords spoke the language of victory.

As the afternoon dragged on, the Linnan attack was being held everywhere. The box, still dripping, was delivered from the palace about three. Since there was no longer any immediate danger, Czinczar sent a messenger to Meewan. At three-thirty Meewan came in grinning broadly. He was followed by slave Linnans carrying a sedan chair. In the chair, bound hand and foot, was the acting Lord Leader of Linn. There was complete silence as the chair was set down, and the slaves withdrew.

Clane studied the barbarian leader with genuine interest. Lady Lydia's opinion of the man had impressed him more than he cared to admit. The question was, could this strong, fine-looking military genius be panicked into thinking that the atom gods existed? Panicked now, during the next half hour? Fortunately, for the first time in his career as an atomic scientist, he had behind him the greatest power ever

185

developed by the wizards of the fabulous days of the legends. He saw that the impersonal expression on the other's face was transforming into the beginning of contempt.

"By the god pits," said Czinczar in disgust, "you Linnans are all the same—weaklings every one."

Clane said nothing. He had looked often with regret into mirrors that showed him exactly what Czinczar was seeing: A slim, young man with a face that was white and womanish and...well, it couldn't be helped.

Czinczar's face changed again. There was suddenly irony in it. "I am speaking," he asked politely, "to Lord Clane Linn? We have not made a mistake?"

Clane couldn't let the opening pass. "No mistake," he said quietly. "I came into Linn for the sole purpose of talking to you while the battle was on. And here I am."

It must have sounded ridiculous, coming from a man bound as he was. The near guards guffawed, and Meewan giggled. Only Czinczar showed no sign. And his marvelous voice was as steady as steel as he said: "I have not the time to flirt with words, nor the inclination. I can see that you are counting on something to save you, and I presume it has something to do with your knowledge of atomic energy."

He fingered the rod of force suggestively. "So far as I can see, we can kill you in less than a second whenever we desire."

Clane shook his head. "You are in error. It is quite impossible for you to kill me."

There was a sound from Meewan. The engineer came forward. "Czinczar," he said darkly, "this man is intolerable. Give me permission to slap his face, and we shall see if his atom gods protect him from indignity."

Czinczar waved him aside. But he stared down at the prisoner with eyes that were abnormally bright. The swiftness with which tension had come into the room amazed him. And, incredibly, it was the prisoner who had seized the advantage—"Impossible to kill me!" In one sentence he dared them to make the attempt.

There was a crinkle of frown in Czinczar's forehead. He had been careful in his handling of Clane as a matter of common sense, not because he actually anticipated disaster. But now, quite frankly, he admitted to himself that the man was not reacting normally. The words Clane had spoken had a ring in them, a conviction that could no longer be ignored. The purpose of his own invasion of the Linnan empire could be in danger.

He said urgently, "I have something to show you. No attempt will be made to kill you until you have seen it. For your part, do nothing hasty, take no action, whatever power you have, until you have gazed with understanding."

He was aware of Meewan giving him an astounded glance. "Power!" exclaimed the designer, and it was like a curse. "The power *he* has!"

Czinczar paid no attention. This was his own special secret, and there could be no delay.

"Guards," he sad, "bring that box over here."

It was soaking wet when they brought it. It left a dirty trail of water on the priceless rug, and a pool began to accumulate immediately in the place where it was set down. There was a delay while sweating men pried off the top. Even the guards at far doors strained to see the contents. A gasp of horror broke the tension of waiting.

What was inside was about eight feet long. Its width was indeterminable, for it seemed to have folds in its body that gave an impression of great size. It had obviously died only a short time before it was packed in the ice. It looked fresh, almost alive, there in its case of ice, unhuman, staring with sightless eyes at the ornate ceiling.

"Where did you get it?" Clane asked at last.

"It was found on one of the moons—within hours after a strange ship was sighted."

"How long ago?" the mutation spoke in a steady tone.

"Two years, Earth time."

"It would seem that whoever was in the ship will have departed by now."

187

Czinczar shook his head. "Miners found a second body exactly like this on a meteorite in a spacesuit—seven months ago."

For a long time, the mutation gazed down at the creature. Finally, he looked, and his eyes met Czinczar's waiting gaze. He said slowly: "What is your theory?"

"A non-human race of great scientific attainments. Ruthless, unfriendly—for there are reports of sudden destruction in outlying areas of Europa which puzzled me until this body was found...I tend to wonder if this might not be a second visitation to the solar system. I cannot give you briefly all the logical relationships I have visualized, but my feeling is that the civilization of the golden age was destroyed by the first visitation."

Clane said: "I am glad that you have shown me this, but what is your purpose in doing so?"

Czinczar drew a deep breath. And made his second move to avert the catastrophe suggested by every action and manner of this unorthodox prisoner. He said: "It would be a grave error for either of us to destroy each other's armies."

"You are asking for mercy?"

That was too strong to take. The barbarian showed his teeth in a snarl. "I am asking for common sense," he said.

"It's impossible," said Clane. "The people must have their revenge. In victory, they will accept nothing less than your death."

The words brought an obscene curse from Meewan. "Czinczar," he shouted, "what is all this nonsense? I have never seen you like this. I follow no man who accepts defeat in advance. I'll show you what we'll do with this...this—" He broke off: "Guards, put a spear into him."

Nobody moved. The soldiers looked uneasily at Czinczar, who nodded coolly. "Go right ahead," he said. "If he can be killed, I'd like to know."

Still nobody moved. It was apparently too mild an order, or something of the leader's tension had communicated to the men. They looked at each other, and they were standing there doubtfully when Meewan snatched a sword from one of them, and turned towards the bound man.

That was as far as he got. Where he had been was a ball of light.

"Try," came the voice of Clane, "to use the rod of force against me." A fateful pause. "Try. It won't kill you."

Czinczar raised the rod of force, and pressed the activator. Nothing happened—Wait! The ball of light was growing brighter.

Clane's voice split the silence tantalizingly. "Do you still not believe in the gods?"

"I am astonished," said Czinczar, "that you do not fear the spread of superstition more than the spread of knowledge. We so-called barbarians," he said proudly, "despise you for your attempt to fence in the human spirit. We are free thinkers, and all your atomic energy will fail in the end to imprison us."

He shrugged. "As for your control over that ball, I do not pretend to understand it."

At last, he had shocked the mutation out of his ice-cold manner. "You actually," said Clane incredulously, "do not believe in the atom gods?"

"Guards," shouted Czinczar piercingly, "attack him from every side."

The ball of light flickered but did not seem to move. There were no guards.

"Now do you believe?" Clane asked.

The barbarian looked haggard and old. But he shook his head. "I have lost the war," he mumbled. "Only that I recognize. It is up to you to take up the mantle which has fallen from my shoulders." He broke off: "What in the name of your gods is that ball?"

"It contains the entire sidereal universe."

Czinczar knit his brow, and leaned forward, as if he were trying to understand.

"The what universe?" he asked at last.

"When you look inside through a hollow tube," Clane

189

explained patiently, "you see stars. It's like a window into space—only it's not a window. It's the universe itself."

The barbarian leader looked genuinely bewildered. "This universe?" he said, blankly.

Clane nodded, but made no comment. It hadn't been easy to grasp so vast an idea, even with the written explanations that he had found.

Czinczar shook his head. "You mean, the Earth is in there?" He pointed at the glowing sphere.

"It's a fourth dimensional idea," said Clane; and still he remained patient. He could recognize a bemused man when he saw one. It was not the moment to press any other point.

The barbarian narrowed his eyes, and said at last: "How can you get a large object into a smaller one?" His tone appealed for a logical explanation.

Clane shrugged. "When largeness or smallness are illusions of viewpoints, the problem does not exist."

Czinczar scowled at that, and straightened. "I have been assuming," he said, "that at this point in our relations you would be speaking nothing but truth. Evidently, you are not prepared to tell me anything valid about your weapon. Naturally, I reject this fanciful story."

Clane shook his head, but said nothing. He had given the only explanation he had, and it had run up against the other man's magnificent realism. Not that he blamed the barbarian. Only gradually had he himself been able to accept the idea that matter and energy were different than they appeared to the sense perceptions of the body.

But now it was time to act, to force, to convince. The bonds fell from him as if they did not exist. He stood up, and now that crown among all the jewels of the ages rode above his head in a matchless perfect rhythm with his movements.

Czinczar said stubbornly, "It would be a mistake to kill any able-bodied man, slave or otherwise."

Clane said, "The gods demand absolute surrender."

Czinczar said in fury, "You fool, I am offering you the

solar system! Has this monster in the box not changed your mind in the slightest degree?"

"It has."

"But then—"

"I do not," said Clane, "believe in joint leadership arrangements."

A pause. Then Czinczar said, "You have come far—who once used atomic power merely to stay alive."

"Yes," said Clane, "I have come far."

Czinczar frowned down at the thing in the box. "The real threat to Linn is there. Will you promise to try for the Lord Leadership?"

"I," Clane said, "can promise nothing."

They looked at each other, two men who almost understood each other. It was Czinczar who broke the silence. "I make an absolute surrender," he said, and it was a sigh, "to you and you alone, of all my forces—in the belief that you have the courage and common sense to shirk none of your new duties as Protector of the Solar System. It was a role," he finished somewhat unnecessarily, suddenly gloomy, "that I originally intended for myself."

In a well-guarded room in a remote suburb of Linn, a core of energy rolled sedately back and forth along a narrow path. In all the solar system there was nothing else like that core. It looked small, but that was an illusion of man's senses. The books that described it, and the men who had written the books, knew but a part of its secrets.

They knew that the micro-universe inside it pulsed with a multiform of minus forces. It reacted to cosmic rays and atomic energy like some insatiable sponge. No sub-molecular energy released in its presence could escape it. And the moment it reached its own strange variation of critical mass it could start a meson chain reaction in anything it touched.

One weakness it had and men had seized upon that in their own greedy fashion. It imitated thought. Or so it seemed. *So it seemed.*

The great question that Clane, and before him the ancients, asked after observing this remarkable characteristic, was: Did this mean that...man controlled the universe, or that the universe controlled man?

About the Author

A. E. van Vogt has been one of the foremost science fiction authors since the late 1930s. A number of his works are considered classics of their kind, including *Slan*, *The World of Null A*, and *The Voyage of the Space Beagle*.

He has also written several memorable series, notably the "Weapon Shops of Isher" novels and the two mutant-mage books, *Empire of the Atom* and its sequel, *The Wizard of Linn*.

His novels are characterized by strong-willed, highly motivated protagonists, who use their physical strength or wits—as well as a keen moral sensibility—to fend off destructive forces that far outnumber them. Van Vogt's work has also been noted for its creative use of new or unusual science-fiction ideas, such as the psychological warfare in *The World of Null A* and the creature in the "Black Destroyer" section of *The Voyage of the Space Beagle*.

Van, as he likes to be called, lives in Los Angeles, where he is working on new books.

Now Available in a Collier Nucleus Edition
The Voyage of the Space Beagle
by A. E. van Vogt

The starship *Space Beagle* is a big ship bound for deep space. With a crew of hundreds, cargo space for a mind-boggling array of alien artifacts and shipments of precious objects, it ventures to planets never before visited by humans, risking destruction and death in its quest for new and unusual experiences.

Only the courage and resourcefulness of the crew stand between them and the perils of the spaceways. And the perils are many, ranging from a creature that can survive for eons in the cold dark vacuum of space, only to regain a power monstrous enough to withstand all the *Space Beagle*'s weaponry, to a mutiny that threatens to destroy the ship from within and lay it open to alien attack.

Through it all, winds the most enthralling, fascinating space adventure that one of science fiction's greatest authors ever wrote.

Great Science Fiction
by Award-Winning Authors
in Collier Nucleus Editions

Helliconia Spring by **Brian W. Aldiss**
One of the greatest epic science fiction novels ever written, a robust adventure set against a vast and colorful world vividly imagined by one of the finest SF authors of all time.

"This is *War and Peace* as distilled through the mind of a troubled futurologist, *Shogun* as penned by a professional visionary."
—*Washington Post Book World*

"A meaty, completely engrossing novel." —*Publishers Weekly*

Helliconia Summer by **Brian W. Aldiss**
It is the middle of a centuries-long summer in the world of Helliconia, as a magnificent drama unfolds. The king of Borlien, beset by enemies, struggles to maintain his power amidst physical and political changes that are sweeping this giant planet. Featuring a colorful swirl of unforgettable characters, the king of Borlien's travails are engrossing, compelling reading.

"This is imaginative science fiction on a major scale, to be compared with the best of the masters in the field." —*St. Louis Post-Dispatch*

The Whole Man by **John Brunner**
Gerald Howson, crippled since birth, uses his extraordinary gift of telepathy to become a "Whole Man" and to heal others who suffer mental anguish and terror. Colorful, powerful science fiction by the Hugo Award–winning author of *Stand on Zanzibar*.

Solar Lottery by **Philip K. Dick**
The psychologically gripping story of an ordinary man caught in a psychic power struggle set in the twenty-third century.

". . . reality and madness, time and death, sin and salvation . . . [Philip K. Dick] is our own homegrown Borges . . ." —Ursula K. Le Guin

Gather, Darkness! by **Fritz Leiber**
Grand Master Fritz Leiber's futuristic tale of high-tech witchcraft involves an idealistic priest who finds himself caught between two warring factions—the all-powerful religious hierarchy and the cult of witches that rises up in opposition.

"A Fritz Leiber book is a real delight."
—Marion Zimmer Bradley, author of *The Mists of Avalon*

A Specter Is Haunting Texas by Fritz Leiber
A politically barbed, post-atomic holocaust novel with the good sense to laugh at itself. Written as a satiric response to the political chaos that swirled around the Vietnam War, it is both a finely crafted science fiction novel of adventure and character and a sharply observed social commentary on the way the United States was torn apart and radicalized during the late 1960s.

Davy by Edgar Pangborn
An extraordinarily powerful, affecting novel of post-holocaust life, by the winner of the International Fantasy Award.

"This is a book of vitality, flowing with wit and originality, where wisdom is wrapped in a chuckle."   —*The Dallas Morning News*

Time and Again by Clifford D. Simak
This is Simak at the top of his form. It combines the deeply humanistic concerns and fast-paced storytelling of Simak the newspaperman with the inventiveness and far-future vision of Simak the science fictioneer. *Time and Again* rivals Isaac Asimov's Robot series in its treatment of robots as the inheritors of our future.

"To read science fiction is to read Simak."   —Robert A. Heinlein

Way Station by Clifford D. Simak
This is the story of Enoch Wallace, a simple farmer who just happens to be a keeper of one of the countless stations of a transit system that spans the galaxy. And now, after millennia of quiet isolation, Enoch's lonely outpost on Earth is fated to become the center of a galaxy-wide crisis, all because of a single act of human kindness.

The Steps of the Sun by Walter Tevis
A twenty-first-century businessman must bring back a new fuel supply and evade government authorities in order to save an energy-depleted earth.

"Engaging and effortless . . . Tevis's best science fiction since *The Man Who Fell to Earth*."   —*Publishers Weekly*

The Year of the Quiet Sun by Wilson Tucker
A time traveler is caught in an American apocalypse at the turn of the twenty-first century. A tale of nuclear war and its survivors.

"Forceful, hard-hitting and, above all, thought-provoking."   —*Locus*

Ask your bookseller for these and other Collier Nucleus Books, or use the order form on the last page of this book to order copies direct.

Other Collier Nucleus titles are available at your local bookstore or by mail. To order directly, return the coupon below to: Macmillan Publishing Company, Special Sales Department, 866 Third Avenue, New York, NY 10022.

Line #	ISBN	Author/Title	Price	Quantity
1	0020160909	ALDISS/Helliconia Spring	$12.00	_____
2	0020160917	ALDISS/Helliconia Summer	$10.00	_____
3	0020302754	BRUNNER/The Whole Man	$ 4.95	_____
4	0020236212	DICK/Solar Lottery	$ 9.00	_____
5	002022348X	LEIBER/Gather, Darkness!	$ 9.00	_____
6	0020223471	LEIBER/A Specter Is Haunting Texas	$ 9.00	_____
7	002035620X	PANGBORN/Davy	$ 4.95	_____
8	0020253958	SIMAK/Time and Again	$ 9.00	_____
9	0020248717	SIMAK/Way Station	$ 8.00	_____
10	002029865X	TEVIS/The Steps of the Sun	$ 4.50	_____
11	0020298951	TUCKER/The Year of the Quiet Sun	$ 4.50	_____
12	0020259905	VAN VOGT/The Voyage of the Space Beagle	$ 8.00	_____

Sub-total _____

Please add postage and handling costs—$2.00 for the first book and 75¢ for each additional book _____

Sales tax—if applicable _____

TOTAL _____

Control No. [   ]   Ord. Type [SPCA]   Lines Units [|]

_____ Enclosed is my check/money order payable to Macmillan Publishing Company.

_____ Bill my _____ AMEX _____ MasterCard _____ Visa   Expiration date _____

Card # _____ Signature _____

Charge orders valid only with signature

Ship to: _____

_____

_____ Zip Code

For charge orders only:

Bill to: _____

_____

_____ Zip Code

For information regarding bulk purchases, please write to Special Sales Director at the above address. Publisher's prices are subject to change without notice. Allow 4–6 weeks for delivery.

FC #1808